Forever Eve

JB LEXINGTON

HADLEIGH HOUSE
PUBLISHING

Hadleigh House Publishing
Minneapolis, MN
www.hadleighhouse.com

Cover art by Gee Gee Collins.
ISBN-13: 978-1-7326347-1-8
ISBN-13: 978-1-7326347-4-9 (ebook)
LCCN: 2020906881

HADLEIGH HOUSE
PUBLISHING

To my loves . . . D-J-B

Forever

Eve

1

Sunlight. I fight the instinct to open my eyes and try to keep my face still. It's useless. I sit up to find Bo lounging on the chaize, reading the morning paper.

Pull yourself together, Izabel. He wants to get help. That's a good sign. There is a process to this kind of healing. We'll work on it together. He'll overcome this. He will. He will.

As I wipe away the tears, I see my wedding dress, a symbol of eternal love and happiness, now a mound of crumpled lace and tulle on the floor. *Yes, he will overcome this. He will.*

"Good morning, baby. I didn't want to wake you too early. You look so peaceful when you sleep." He rises and makes his way to my side of the bed and lingers over me. "I had some coffee brought up." He offers what appears to be an apologetic smile.

I stare up at him, my thoughts a scramble with scenes from last night. Fighting back tears, I reach for the mug. "Thanks."

He gently wraps his hand around mine, bows his head, and releases a big sigh. After a moment, he begins to pace along the edge of the bed. "Izabel, I'm . . . It's just you . . . sometimes you leave me no other choice. I'll talk to someone about . . ." he trails off. "My issues. Forgive me. I will make it right again."

I won't let him see me cry. I have to stay strong, but I know if I answer him, I won't be able to hold back a torrent of tears. I lower my eyes, nod, and hope I look agreeable. He leans down and kisses me on the forehead.

"All right then. I'll leave you to get ready. We're having breakfast with my parents. Meet us in the dining room in a half hour."

The door closes, and I collapse back onto the bed. I turn to my side and cradle one of the pillows to my chest, sobbing raggedly as I reflect on yesterday's events. It was supposed to be the best day of my life. My wedding day.

□ □ □

The Carmichael's have spared no expense. I'm sure they have invited all of Illinois's most influential and affluent dignitaries, politicians, and socialites. It's a *who's who* of potential leads and allies that will help advance Bo's career, or so I've been told. I won't know most of my guests with the exception of a few old friends.

It's a glorious September afternoon. I'm standing in front of the large, ornate mirror that leans against the wall in the bridal party suite of the Waldorf Astoria. I don't recognize the girl staring back.

I'm glad I went with the strapless, lace vintage dress. Vintage always feels so familiar.

All my work at the gym has really paid off. I slimmed down, and the silhouette of the dress flatters my new shape. I achieved my goal of getting down to a size six—well, Bo wanted me to be a size six. The diamond-embellished belt that's tied around my waist is the perfect finish. I look so tiny, and the dress falls elegantly down my hips, snug in all the right spots.

My hair is in loose tendrils down my back, pulled up on one side with a pin and adorned with a delicate cluster of stephanotis flowers. My makeup is light and natural looking, as usual. Too much, Bo says, makes me look like one of those "girls" that hang out on the north side of town, not a future governor's wife. I give myself one final look over and can't help but smile. Yes, Bo will be delighted when he sees me.

Finally—*finally*—this day is here. We've been engaged three very long years. Bo's father was adamant that he needed to establish himself on the political scene before he got married, even though the Carmichaels have a historic political lineage. I don't know how many times I've heard the story about how it all started with Lord Carmichael who served under King George II. From birth, Bo was groomed to carry on his family legacy. The right clothes, the perfect connections, acceptable behavior ingrained into his every thought and motion, into his very public being.

Natalie bursts through the door in her usual bull-in-a-china-shop fashion, snapping me out of my reverie. "All right, as much as it pains me to say this, let's get you married, bitch!" She really needs to work on her graces.

Natalie Spencer is my oldest and dearest friend. We've been inseparable since elementary school, even though we're polar opposites. In high school, I had to work hard to get good grades, my face always in a book, and she could've been working for NASA at the young age of sixteen. But, ever the rebel, she ran with the emo crowd. The only thing we had in common back then was that we were both growing up without a father. Somehow, it was enough for us. We knew we would have a life-long connection.

Natalie is tall and naturally slim with ridiculous curves she doesn't even have to work for. The kind of woman who could make a garbage bag look trendy, she keeps her short, dark-brown hair a perfect rock 'n' roll mess on top of her head. Any time of the day or night, that hair is ready to party.

Nothing makes her happier than booze, blow, boys, and boobs. She makes no excuses and never apologizes for her chosen lifestyle. Natalie has accomplished so much in her life, and I secretly admire her. I would never tell her, because one of us has to be the responsible one in this friendship, but I suspect she knows.

She is openly bisexual. Her words: *Love is love, regardless of what's below the belt.*

We tried to fool around once a few years back after too many glasses of pinot grigio, but halfway through I started giggling and couldn't stop. I like cock too much to ever be a lesbian. That's according to Nat's crude theory. I never told Bo. He was raised in an ultra-conservative and religious household. Me, not so much. The only time I heard my mom reference Jesus was when something went wrong, and it was usually followed by an expletive. I respect Bo's opinions and values, though, and deep down he's just a big softy. He's also drop-dead gorgeous, which I don't mind one bit.

"Izabel Jones, aren't you a vision of the oppression of women, all dressed in white."

"Nice, Nat! How many mimosas have you had already?" I try to sound offended, but it's impossible in the face of her *joie de vivre*.

"Come on, Jones. It's your wedding day. Let's have some fun. Look, I'm even wearing a bra for you." She flashes me her lace-covered boob with her free hand. The other is occupied by two glasses of champagne and orange juice. She gestures for me to take one of the long-stemmed flutes from her.

"Nat, you know Bo's not keen on me drinking."

"Bo, Shmo . . . He's so boring . . . You never have fun anymore." She pushes out her lower lip in a pout and thrusts a glass at me.

"One drink, Nat, and that's it."

She raises hers, and with her worst, uppity British accent, she toasts, "To the future Mrs. Bo Carmichael. May all your champagne wishes and caviar dreams come true."

"Robin Leach, really!" I giggle, we clink glasses, and we take a long sip.

My mother walks in the room and eyes us suspiciously. "You two look like you're up to no good."

In the twenty years we've been friends, Natalie has never become my mother's favorite person, but my mother tolerates her. My mom has always wanted the best for me. She was a single parent working too many hours, determined I would get more out of life than she did. She always said I deserved to marry a rich man to take care of me so I wouldn't have to work as hard as she did and miss out on the grand privileges of life. Natalie, of course, would never let a man take care of her, so to my mother, Nat was always just an obstacle in her chosen path for me.

"Izabel, you look beautiful. Bo is going to be so pleased!" She gives me a loose hug so as to not pull at my dress. When Mom lets go, she holds me at arm's length, scanning me from head to toe before giving me an approving smile. "Oh, honey, I'm so happy for you. You are going to have a wonderful life. You'll never have to worry about anything." If she had a choice, I think *she'd* be marrying Bo today.

Natalie looks at me and rolls her eyes, and I give her the don't-start stare.

"Okay, sweetheart." Mom's voice is a sing-song testament to her happiness. "Let's get you married!"

Natalie watches me take a final sip of my drink and flashes me one of her signature smiles, her right boob again evoking an eye roll from my mom this time. Mom and I are alone in the room now for my last few single-girl moments before we make our way down the hall to the chapel room.

With nerves of delight coursing through me, Mom and I stand arm in arm waiting for the doors to open. On cue, two impeccably dressed men in full tuxedos and white gloves open the double doors. The low buzz of several hundred guests murmuring among themselves greets us as we step into the room. The guests stand, and Mom and I start our slow march to the altar where my future husband waits. I float down the aisle to the euphoric melody being played by the string quartet tucked away in the corner.

All I see is Bo's sweet, genuine smile. He's fiddling with the boutonniere on his lapel. He looks as nervous as I feel. Man, he is gorgeous. He's wearing a tailored, charcoal pinstripe suit that drapes without flaw over his 6'3" frame. His blond hair is tousled to perfection. *And he's all mine.*

In a blur, we move from being two single people to man and wife. With Reverend Wallace's, "You may now kiss your bride," Bo grabs me, dips me down low, and plants a long, deep kiss on my lips. The guests applaud and cheer around us. He stands me back up, steadies me, grabs my hand, and we walk toward the exit amidst smiles and congratulations. When the doors close on the guests behind us, Bo takes me in his arms and swings me around.

"Well hello, Mrs. Carmichael." He flashes me his perfect smile.

"Hello yourself, Mr. Carmichael. Why don't we take a quick detour to our room before the party starts?"

His smile fades. "Izabel, we have guests waiting for us."

I pout and give him my biggest doe eyes. "You can deviate from your schedule just this once, Bo."

He wraps his hand around my forearm, squeezes, and jerks me toward him. I gasp. "We can't deviate from the schedule, Izabel. Do you understand?"

I look up at him, and he softens his grip then pulls me into an embrace. I tense up as he hugs me.

"I'm sorry." His whisper blows the loose tendrils of hair away from my ear. For a moment, he regards me, his face expressionless. "Come on, darling. Let's go have a good night with our guests. I'll make it up to you later." And with the flash of his pearly whites, I melt a bit and let it go *again*.

Bo and I spend the rest of the night floating from table to table, greeting our guests, most of whom I'm meeting for the first time. For the most part, I listen in a daze, smiling and accepting their congratulations. I don't have much to offer when it comes to politics. I guess I'll have to work on that now that I'm the wife of the future governor of Illinois.

A shriek jolts me to attention. "Are you kidding me?"

I whip my head around, recognizing Nat's voice. Bo glares down at me with a get-her-the-fuck-out-of-here look. I excuse myself and rush over to where she is standing. She's holding her champagne flute in one hand and gesticulating furiously with the other. I smile sweetly at the two elderly gentlemen Natalie has clearly outraged.

"What's going on?" I whisper through clenched teeth and a fake smile.

"I'll tell you what's going on. These two fuckers have just informed me that homosexuality is a sin, and any man or woman who decides to become gay will live in eternal damnation. What the fuck, Jones?"

"Nat!" I hiss at her. With a quick apology to the men, I grab Natalie by the arm and usher her toward the door. Without even looking at him, I can *feel* Bo's angry glare on my back as we exit the room. I'll have to deal with that later.

I get Natalie into the hallway and duck into a utility room off to the side. "What the hell, Nat?"

"I'm sorry, Jones. I didn't know your hubby invited neo-Nazis to the reception and I would be subjected to this bullshit."

"Why can't you just keep your opinions to yourself for, like, ten minutes?" Then, a bit softer, but still firmly, I say, "It's my wedding day. *Please* don't make Bo angry."

She stares at me for a long while and opens her mouth to say something but decides against it. She leans in, gives me a hug, and then kisses my cheek.

"Anything for you, Jones." She holds out her hand. "Come on, let's go party."

I let out a big sigh in hopes I've just defused one of Bo's blowups. Hand in hand, we walk back into the reception. I smile and laugh and make my rounds with an unsettling prickling on the back of my neck.

The evening continues in much the same way I imagine most girls dream their wedding will be. I'm sitting at a table with some college friends, giving my sore feet a much-needed break. What made me think I could last eight hours in my mile-high Louboutins?

I watch Bo across the room, working his magic, wooing our most prominent guests. He looks the way a man should on his wedding night: overjoyed at the notion of spending endless days and nights with the love of his life. He sees me admiring him and starts the slow progression toward me, one handshake and bout of small talk at a time. When he reaches the table, he offers me his wide, flat hand. Even it is beautiful.

"Will you dance with me, Mrs. Carmichael?"

"I thought you'd never ask, Mr. Carmichael."

He leads me to the dance floor and pulls me close.

We start to sway to the sweet sound of Etta James, and he lip-syncs the lyrics, "*At last, my love has come along... lonely days are over.*"

I'm suspended—just like that—in his arms, inches from the ground when he dips me low and brushes a feather-light kiss on my lips. Somewhere, seemingly so far from here, our guests applaud around us. He swoops me up and twirls me around the dance floor a few times. The applause grows louder. When I'm steadied back in his arms, I look up to meet his eyes, but he's not looking at me at all.

It's one a.m. when we finally make our way down the hallway to our suite. Exhaustion has set in, and I cling to Bo's arm for support. My Louboutins are twisted through my fingers in my other hand. I can't believe I survived the entire day and night without taking them off.

Beauty and comfort are not synonymous when it comes to designer footwear.

The tension between me and Bo is palpable. I suspect he's stewing about Natalie's outburst now that he doesn't have the distractions of our guests. His silent treatment is ridiculous. It's our wedding night. We should be drunk on happiness and whirling in the anticipation of making love as newlyweds.

Pulling his hand up to my mouth, I kiss his knuckles and gush, "What a day! It was like the perfect fairy tale. Everything went off without a hitch."

"Not entirely," he grumbles and opens the door to the suite. I open my mouth to rebut, but decide it's to my benefit to keep my comments to myself.

The room is beautiful and spacious. An oversized

floral arrangement of my favorites— magnolias and freesia—are on the dining table, and there is a silver platter of chocolate-dipped strawberries and a bottle of champagne chilling in an ice bucket. "Oh, Bo, look how beautif—"

The word is lost in a gasp as my shoulders make contact with the wall. He's up against me with the full force of his weight, forcing his tongue into my mouth like venom from a snake.

"Bo, please, not like this. Not tonight." My voice is little more than a whisper as I use my forearms to gain an inch of space. "We're married now. We've been waiting for this night for so long. Make love to me."

He looks up at the ceiling, his frustration apparent. "Turn around."

The vibration of his growl galvanizes me. He knots my hair in his hand and pulls hard to one side. He buries his face in my neck and bites down until I can feel the skin break. With his free hand, he unzips my dress, and it falls to the floor like a deflated balloon. I hear the quick, practiced undoing of his belt and fly: *clink, zip*. Silent tears roll down my cheeks.

"Bo, *please*."

"Shhhh." He grunts. "Spread your legs." He pulls my white silk panties to the side and takes me. It's devoid of any love. I know that.

In a minute, he'll press my face into a pillow, and I'll drift to that serene place in the back of my mind where we make passionate love and punishment fucks don't exist.

□ □ □

2

I enter the dining room exactly half an hour later with renewed confidence, wearing my new Michael Kors Jersey dress and Espadrille wedges. My hair is a bit frizzy, but presentable enough after brushing out the curls from yesterday—the only thing I could do with only a half hour to get ready.

I spot Mrs. Carmichael waving me over. She likes to be called Tippy, though her birth name is Patricia. I think there's a story behind the nickname, but it has never been offered to me, and I haven't asked. If there is anything I've learned about the Carmichaels over the years, it's you don't ask questions, just follow instructions. She's petite with golden blonde hair perfectly coiffed, and she's always so composed in her fitted, designer suits.

"We're over here, darling." She's standing now and waving her linen napkin at me.

Tippy's flare for the over dramatic can be a lot to take at times, but always seems genuine with me. Given that she's a politician's wife, I suspect she needs to be a bit guarded and isn't genuine with most people. When I reach the table, she gives me a gentle hug, air-kissing either side of my cheeks.

"You look lovely, Izabel. Married life certainly agrees with you." Her cordial greeting is accompanied by a full glance up and down my body.

Bo and Mr. Carmichael stand to greet me as well. Bo's dad gives me a clipped "good morning" accompanied by an uncomfortable hug that lasts a few seconds too long. He's always been indifferent toward me. I think he secretly hoped Bo would marry a girl with a more influential family name, like Bush or Reagan.

I sit in my assigned place, and Bo pushes my chair in for me. He leans down and whispers in my ear, "You look gorgeous, Izabel Carmichael." With a subtle brush of my hair to the side, he gently kisses the imprint that remains on my neck from last night's strike.

Instinctively, I tense, but manage a feeble smile. *He said he was sorry, Izabel. Just relax.*

I appraise the buffet of dishes that have already been delivered to the table. The food is impeccably plated, but my stomach is heavier than a brick. There is juice and coffee, and Tippy has her signature pitcher of her go-to drink in front of her.

"Izabel, darling, let me pour you a drink. They make the perfect Bloody Mary here." She smiles and waves her glass at me.

"No, thank you." I decline as graciously as I can. "I'll eat some breakfast first." To make it seem true, I shovel some cantaloupe onto my plate.

Tippy dives in about her latest charitable endeavors and lists the events she'd like me to attend. She once told me, "Darling, a Carmichael lady has to be omnipresent, look opulent, and appear sober at all times."

I turn my attention to the men's conversation when I hear them talking about our honeymoon.

"But we've already discussed this, Dad. These arrangements were made months ago." Bo's face is turning ever so slightly pink.

Mr. Carmichael holds his hand up to interject. "Bo, I told you plans might need to change. The agenda over the next few weeks is too important, and your absence will be detrimental to the campaign. We can't allow these Limousine Liberals to get a leg up on us." He pauses and takes a sip of his coffee. "Plus, you kids are young. You have plenty of time to travel."

Not go on our honeymoon? He can't be serious. It isn't fair. He has no right to dictate this too. I hold up my glass and look at Tippy. "On second thought, I'll have that drink now."

Tippy's eyes sparkle and her half grin turns to a beaming smile as she tips the pitcher into my glass. I take two big, unladylike gulps. *Wow, this does taste good...* She gives me a wink, and I know it's because she recognizes my bridled fury.

My poor Bo. He looks so defeated. He'd never question his father's tactics. He aches too much for his approval and love. A glint of light shines off my ring. I'm his wife. He needs my support. I need to speak up.

"Mr. Carmichael, with all due respect, Bo has been working nonstop for months. The reason we delayed the wedding and the honeymoon"—I want to shout *for the last three years*—"was so he could dedicate more time to the campaign."

Tippy's head bobs like a buoy, up at me, down at her plate. Even Bo won't meet my eye.

Mr. Carmichael snorts and gives me an amused look. "Listen, darlin', I don't expect you to understand what this business entails. You just keep looking pretty, and Tippy will let you know when you're needed and what events to attend."

Bo's fingers grip mine and vise close before he lets go. Tippy hails the waiter and, ever so quietly, regards me over the rim of her glass with what seems to be a supportive wink.

Outside the hotel now, I continue to bite my tongue as I hear Jack mumbling political whatevers to Bo. Thomas, the driver, holds the door open for Tippy and she slides into the back seat of the vintage white Bentley. He's decked out in a three-piece suit, a hat, and white gloves. The Carmichaels come from old money, and they make sure nobody forgets it. Jack waits on the other side of the car for Thomas to come open his door as well and leaves us with a goodbye nod. "Bo, don't forget what we discussed," he barks and then disappears into the car.

After Bo's parents drive off, we wait in silence for what seems an eternity for the valet to bring our car around. I can actually see the pre-fall leaves on the London plane trees changing color. Bo gently wraps his fingers around mine. The torment that is Jack Carmichael is tangible. I wish Bo would let me in. He's so guarded when it comes to his father. We're in this together now. I'll be his supportive wife and do what I can to avoid adding unneeded stress. Sure, it would be wonderful to wake up early tomorrow morning, roll over, kiss my husband, and say, "It's time to get up, baby." Hop in the town car, airport bound. Just me and him thousands of miles away, being lazy all day, sun tanning on the beach. Maybe do some snorkeling or scuba diving. My clothes were picked out last week and packed by outfit. I bought a new baby blue bikini and sandals as a surprise for Bo; baby blue is his favorite color. If postponing our time in paradise helps Bo deal with his father, then that's what we'll do. His dad isn't wrong. We're young. We have a long future together, and we'll have to work on being better to carve out time for us. All part of being married: compromise and communicate. I squeeze Bo's hand as a gesture of my love and support.

"Seriously! Where is the fucking car?" Bo huffs. "This place has really gone to shit."

I choose not to respond. My phone pings. It's a text from Natalie.

"Who's that?" His tone suggests impatience, but his expression gives no clue as to why.

Unsure of what his reaction will be, timidly I say, "Oh it's just Nat."

"What does she want?" is his gruff response.

"She wants us to meet her tomorrow night. Some art thing."

"Not going," he responds immediately.

"What? Why?" I'm vexed and puzzled. "Bo, I know some of Natalie's friends aren't your scene, but it could be fun. It will be our first function out as a married couple." Pausing for his response, I catalogue my thoughts so I can choose my words carefully, but he says nothing.

"It's okay, just forget I mentioned it. I'll just go on my own. You're busy and have a lot on your plate with work and with Jack—I mean, your father." My feeble attempt to back pedal is making me feel uneasy.

"Izabel, we're not going. Also, I'm leaving on business in the morning," he says.

"So soon?" The disappointment in my voice is undeniable. "Is that what you and your dad were talking about before?"

"Yes."

This conversation is going from bad to worse. *You can do this, Izzy. Deflect his mood. Turn this around and bring Bo back. Remember: compromise and communicate.*

"Great, now I don't have to feel bad leaving my new husband home alone." I poke at his side and flash him a big smile, hoping an injection of levity will change the curve this subject is taking us on.

He lets out an audible sigh, drops my hand, then turns and faces me.

"Izabel. Maybe you didn't hear me. Read my lips. You. Are. Not. Going."

My body tenses and I take a small step back, leaning away from him. He must realize how forceful he sounds. Bo pulls me quickly into one of his signature bear-hugs that always make me feel like a giant has just cradled me.

"Besides, now you'll have time to yourself to get back to the decorating changes in the house you had talked about. It's all yours, baby, my gift to you. You can choose the colors, the furniture, and the tapestries. All of it. Whatever your heart desires." He hugs me tighter to reinforce his words. "Anything for my baby." He drops his lips onto mine and offers a gentle kiss.

Well, he's not wrong. I've been so wrapped up with all the wedding plans this last year, I haven't had an extra minute to do much else, let alone think about redecorating.

The valet arrives with the car. One thing I can say about Bo is he's a gentleman. He always holds the door open for me. Once I hear the sound of the door, I let out a big sigh. *Regroup, Izzy.*

Our ride home is quiet. I'm not bothered by that. The silence is appreciated, actually. The tension from earlier hovers over me like a construction crane carrying a load of concrete.

A wave of relief floods over me when we pull into the driveway. When we're back in our house and settled, Bo will retreat to his office and I can sink into my soaker tub and wash away the angst from the last twelve hours.

Unconcerned by my familiar surroundings, I walk up to the front door as I've done countless times since we moved in. But I'm startled by the swift move of being tossed over Bo's shoulder. His laugh is hearty, and he playfully smacks at my bottom.

"What are you doing?" I shriek, partly with joy and partly with trepidation.

"I have to carry my new bride over the threshold," he proclaims.

Instantly, my body succumbs to the moment of celebration and I enjoy the jaunt to the front door.

He fumbles with the key but finally unlocks the door and takes the stairs two at a time until he reaches the top landing of the second floor. Without stopping, he heads straight to our bedroom and tosses me on the bed. Gently now, he straddles me and rests his forehead on my chest. The sound of the sigh he releases is that of agony.

"Izabel. You have to know how sorry I am. I hate that I acted like such an asshole. He . . . he just makes me turn into something—someone I don't want to be."

I cradle his head in my hands and guide him to look at me. "Listen to me. I know you, Bo Carmichael. We'll get through this together. Let's promise each other, please." I plant a tender kiss on his left cheek and then another on his right.

"You're so good to me, and I'm . . . well, I'm nothing without you." He pauses. "I have a great idea. I'm going to run a bath for you and pour you a glass of champagne. You are officially a Carmichael woman and deserve to be treated like one."

3

When I walk through the front door, I kick my shoes into the pile that has collected over the last couple of days. As I sulk down the hallway, I notice the heap of bags on the floor and another of jackets and sweaters on the dining table. This is so not like me. Who can blame me, though? It's lonely in this big house when Bo is away. When I reach the living room, I slouch down onto the couch and look around. There's more mess than any Carmichael wife in her right mind would ever allow.

Turtle Island. It's out there. Somewhere. Somewhere Bo and I are not. Three glorious weeks of honeymoon—I can see them blur before my eyes, a mirage where we are alone, far from reality, and I have Bo's undivided attention—so, so far away from Jack Carmichael. I'm beginning to think Bo's dad doesn't have his best interests at heart. I've learned all too well it's best to refrain from mentioning Jack in any of our discussions.

So, here I am, at home alone for the third weekend in a row since our wedding. The Carmichael men are away again. I think it's Texas today. Bo used to leave me itineraries for all of his trips, but now he says they're too inconsistent and he doesn't want to bother me with all the changes. He says I have my own busy schedule and I shouldn't have to worry about his.

Tippy's apathetic words—*get used to it, dear*—play over and over in my head.

I flip from one side of the couch to the other. I can't get comfortable. *Maybe I'll watch TV.* I reach for the remote under the stack of magazines on the side table, and everything goes crashing to the ground. I really need to clean up. Maybe I should get a cleaning lady, like Bo suggested.

My mother would have a heart attack if she found out someone else was cleaning my house. Sure, she wanted me to marry into a wealthy family, but she would find it disgraceful if another woman picked up after me. My mother didn't even do that while I was growing up. I was responsible for half the chores around the house. Even when she worked two jobs, our house was always spotless.

I bend down to grab the remote from under the pile on the floor and notice the memory album I put together for our rehearsal dinner party. That's strange. Was Bo looking through it? It's a sweet thought, seeing as he wanted nothing to do with it when I was assembling it.

It was supposed to be a fun project for us to do together, a little walk down memory lane.

He was under so much stress in the weeks leading up to the wedding, I thought he'd be happy remembering our simpler times. I wouldn't let up. I wanted him to be involved. He said I was insinuating he had changed, and he was sick of everyone breathing down his neck, telling him what to do and how to act.

He hadn't meant to hit me with it. I shouldn't have pulled it away from him. He was only trying to get me to listen to his point of view. My poor Bo, he's so conflicted. Our lives would have been so different if he had just followed his own dreams. Law is his passion. He should be teaching at the University of Chicago. When we first started dating, it was all he talked about. I was so young and naive then and didn't know the first thing about relationships. Who does at twenty-two?

I open the front cover of the book and start to laugh. It's the photo of Bo and me on our first weekend away together. We were eating lobster, and Bo hooked the claw onto his nose as if he'd been snapped. I'd spit wine across the table, all over his face. I was mortified. He was so good about it. He wiped his face and attached another claw to his earlobe.

We had gone to a quaint little B&B in Maine. Every other couple staying there must have been seventy years old. We didn't mind, though. It was ... peaceful. There was something familiar, even comforting, listening to their stories about the good old days.

With every flip of the page, more wonderful memories emerge. Bo and I skiing in Aspen, us at New Year's Eve parties, blowing our horns. I start to laugh again when I see the pictures of me soaked like a drowned rat while we camped in the pouring rain. I detest camping, but he wanted to try it, so I went along.

Here's the ticket stub from the concert on the night I met Bo. He wasn't actually *there*. It was yet another night

Natalie dragged me out. There was some new band out at the time that was a big hit with the lesbian crowd. She made me go as a buffer. I was her "girlfriend" when the girls she wasn't interested in approached her, but I was to beat it if one came around she wanted to pursue. And when that girl did come along—and of course, she did—I ended up on the street, hailing a cab home.

I didn't go home though, because out in front of the adjacent club was a group of guys hanging out, laughing, and catcalling, all except for one. He came over to excuse his friends' behavior. He towered over me, his blue eyes apologetic and kind. I couldn't look away. He asked me if I wanted to go for coffee and dessert, and I accepted.

It took less than five minutes after our coffee to see that Blue Eyes thought that while catcalling was wrong, not putting out after he'd dropped all of twelve dollars on our lattes and ice cream was a far worse crime. He locked his arms around me and grabbed a handful of my ass. I squirmed, looking for anyone to help me out of his virile clutch. Then I heard a voice behind me. "Hey man, I don't mean to interrupt, but this chick? Herpes."

"Ah, fuck."

And just like that, he was gone.

I whirled around, appalled to be mistaken as "Herpes Chick," then I saw the face attached to the mystery voice, and I knew he'd saved me. We've been together every day since.

Now that I feel warm and fuzzy again, maybe I'll give him a call to say, "I love you." I take my phone out of my pocket to dial, and I see a text from Natalie:

Yo Bo-fo ... Haha. I just made that up. No wonder you love me. I'm hilarious. You still good to go out Tuesday?

I reply, *Yup*.

My phone pings almost immediately with a reply.

Yay! I'll meet you at your work. We'll decide where to go then. Ciao ciao.

I haven't seen Natalie since the wedding. I needed Bo to cool down after her little incident. Plus, I wouldn't have been able to sneak my troubles past her. I knew she would be able to tell something wasn't right with me. There's no way I could've told her about what happened after the wedding. She would've gone ballistic. She still would, but she won't notice. She'll be distracted by other things. She's always been what I call a "butterfly chaser," and I've always been the rock.

We did a prick-your-finger blood pact when we were twelve. We saw it in a movie once, and she thought it would be a good idea, until we both ended up at the hospital getting a tetanus shot because Natalie said the nail she found on her garage floor would be fine to use. And somehow, even as an adult, I still listen to her.

I dial Bo, but it just rings and goes to voice mail. Why does this man never answer his phone? How many damn meetings can there be?

"Hi. It's me, just saying hi. I'll see you after work tomorrow. I'll show you how much I've missed you. Love you. Bye." That should put him in a good mood for tomorrow. Bo loves frisky me.

As soon as I hang up, the home phone rings. That's odd. Nobody but Tippy ever calls the landline.

Frantically, I look for the cordless receiver. "Hello?"

"Izabel, darling. You sound out of breath."

"Tippy. What's wrong? Is Bo all right?"

"Yes, of course." Her clipped tone suggests she's dismissing my concern. "Listen, darling. I've just spoken with Jack's assistant, and we are required at a function tomorrow evening. I'll send the car around to get you at six-thirty p.m. sharp."

"But what about Bo?"

"What about him?"

"Will he be there?" Hope cracks my voice.

"Yes, they will meet us there. It's cocktail attire, so dress accordingly. If you need anything, I can have Damien send something from the boutique. *Do* you need something?" She's more curt than usual. Damien is Tippy's personal assistant. I'm not sure why she needs one, but I stopped questioning anything about that family a long time ago.

"I'll be fine, thanks. I'll see you tomorrow."

"Goodbye, darling."

□ □ □

The next evening, at six-thirty on the dot, there's a knock at the front door.

I look far better than I feel. Tippy has given me enough advice for the dress code at these functions—modesty, always modesty—nothing above the knee, muted solid colors. Cap sleeves are as much shoulder as we can expose, and forget about showing any cleavage. I might as well have the devil's tattoo across my chest. Not that I make it a habit of showing off the girls, but something about being told what to wear all the time is unnerving—no, annoying.

I go with my black cocktail dress that flairs out just below the knee. It has a lovely, asymmetrical neckline and a thin, black patent belt. Tippy doesn't have any rules about shoes, so I've put on my favorite Mary-Jane peep-toe Louboutins. There is inexplicable power in those red soles. Every woman should own a pair.

I open the door to find a man standing with a large bouquet of flowers hiding his face, like a painting by René Magritte. Obviously, they are from Bo, but he never sends flowers. This is such a nice, unexpected surprise. I'm awe-struck and begin to giggle like a young schoolgirl getting her first passed love note.

"I'm sorry. Where are my manners? Let me take these from you." As I reach for the flowers, the man exposes his face. It's Bo. My Bo, home at last. I squeal with excitement and jump into his arms, squishing the flowers between us.

He breaks into spirited laughter. "Easy! I put a lot of thought into these." He has such a great laugh. I remember when he used to laugh all the time.

"But I thought . . . your mom said . . ."

"I know you've been upset with me about the honeymoon not working out, and I wanted to do something nice for you. Plus, I got your message. I think I'd like to take you up on that offer." He leans down and crushes his lips against mine.

"Bo, you have no idea how much this means to me. I love you. You're going to want to go away all the time when I'm finished with you tonight."

He frowns slightly. I'm sure he feels bad about having to travel so much. Regardless, my Bo is back.

"Let me put these in some water, then we can go." I motion to take the flowers from him.

"No, we don't have time. Put them on the table and deal with them later." He shoves them into my hands rather urgently. I'm not sure what's triggered this change, but I don't argue, and instead, drop the bouquet on the table and head out the door.

Thankfully, the event doesn't last long. We're back in the comfort of our home before eleven. But my night isn't finished yet. I have plans for my husband.

"How about a nightcap?" The innocence in my voice betrays the burning passion in my stomach.

"It's late, Izabel, and we both have to be up early."

I'm undeterred. It's not unusual after events like this for him to need a while to come down from the shop talk.

Slowly I uncurl one finger up and cast an uninhibited smile through my eyes

" Fine. Just one." A grin creeps across his lips.

I skip off to the kitchen, and Bo heads into the living room. I've been planning this all night. I take down two snifters from the cabinet and fill them halfway with cognac. It smells delicious. I'm not even sure I like cognac, but I've seen Bo drink it, and it seems like the perfect drink for seducing one's husband.

I take off my dress and fold it neatly on the counter. I purposely wore my black lace set and thigh-highs. And, of course, as with any good seduction, the shoes stay on. When I walk back into the living room, Bo's cradling his head in his hands.

"Hey, are you okay?" My voice is filled with concern. I've never seen him look this vulnerable.

"Wow. You look so beautiful. I've done nothing to deserve you." His response sounds more like a confession than a compliment.

I approach when he holds his hand out, inviting me closer to him. Reluctantly, I straddle his lap. His uneasiness is tangible. My earlier vision of straddling him was much more sensual. I hand him a glass then take a sip from my own. It burns going down, but it's good. I hope a few sips will lighten the mood. Bo knocks his back in one swift gulp.

"Bo, what's wrong? Don't you like my outfit?" I snap the strap of my bra, hoping my levity will break him out of desolation.

"It's nothing. I was just thinking what a lucky man I am."

I ignore my own feelings of unease and kiss him. He responds hurriedly. There hasn't been passion like this between us for so long. My glass clanks onto the side table. He stands with me still wrapped around him, then plants me on the couch. The weight of his body is almost suffocating, but I want him—no, I *need* him. He puts his face in my neck then kisses furiously down to my chest, pulling my breast out of the cup of my bra and nibbling my nipple, sending spikes of pleasure between my thighs. I moan and dig my nails into his back through his shirt.

He pulls at my other breast, but bites harder this time, making me cry out. I feel his hand drop down between my legs. The lace from my panties rubs against me, adding to the sensation as he moves his fingers around my clitoris. With one swift tug, he snaps the delicate string holding the panties together. I gasp as he quickly sinks two fingers deep inside me. I move with them as they slide in and out.

His mouth finds mine and he unleashes a rampage of carnal kisses. Is it going to be like . . . ? No, there's something more behind these kisses. He needs me to love him this way right now.

I hear the clink of his buckle and the zipper of his pants and grab his face with my hands, grateful for the lewd invasion of his tongue. His hard cock sweeps up my wetness before he slams into me.

"Oh, that feels so good." I groan and push up onto him. I need to feel him deeper inside me.

"I love you, Izabel." He continues thrusting, deep and slow. My insides tingle. I tilt my pelvis to find friction for my clitoris and begin to gyrate.

"Fuck me hard, Bo." My whisper is what I hope seduction sounds like.

He halts mid-thrust. "Why would you say that?" His eyes frost over, the passion fading.

Stirring with pleasure, but concerned by his reaction, I struggle to speak. "What's wrong?"

"You're my wife, not some slut I fuck."

"Bo, we were in the moment. I just said it. You haven't minded before." I grab for his face to pull him in for a kiss, but he turns away.

He pulls out and stands. Fastening his pants, he completely ignores me, muttering something under his breath. He reaches to the side table, picks up my unfinished glass of cognac, and shoots it back. I lie there half-naked, goose bumps forming on my arms.

"Bo. Look at me. What . . . what have I done wrong?"

"Nothing. Forget about it." His voice is low and flat.

I can't do anything but lie there in the face of this rejection. What is wrong with me? First, I don't show enough interest, now I've shown too much? What is wrong with our marriage?

I watch the back of his head, bowed low, as he skulks away down the hall. When is it safe to follow? What can I say to fix this?

He is already buried under the duvet when I walk into the bedroom. I remove what little I have on and climb in beside him. I don't want him going to sleep thinking I'm angry at him.

Snuggling up behind him, I thread my arm under his, around to his front. He stiffens at first then relaxes after a few seconds. He takes my hand in his and gives it a little reassuring squeeze, for both of us, I think.

4

My days meld together in endless cycles of eating and sleeping, attending political functions, shaking hands, forcing fake smiles, and making small talk with other robot wives. I'm starting to forget who I am. I need a run. I need to sweat.

"Earth to Jones." Natalie's sharp tone snaps me out of my silence. "What's going on with you? Seriously. Where have you *been*? You've canceled our last few lunch dates, and you never call me anymore. It's a miracle you even came to dinner—and I don't believe in miracles!

You're not still mad about Wedding Gate, are you?"

"No, Nat, I'm fine. I'd never stay mad at you. Besides, your outburst was one of the highlights of the night." We giggle, but I'm stifled all too quickly by the unwelcome memory of that night in our honeymoon suite.

Nat has no idea what her actions cost me. I shake my head to clear my thoughts. Natalie's like a human lie detector. If I look her in the eyes, she will know something is wrong. Since we were young, she's been able to read me like a book.

"Listen, Nat, I have something I want to talk—" My sentence is cut short by her screech.

"Oh my God. I almost forgot to tell you about my, err, our latest enlightenment!"

"What are you trying to drag me into now?" She is exhausting sometimes, but I'm kind of relieved by her interruption. I'm not sure I'm ready to tell her what's been going on with Bo.

"Just listen, Jones. It's called PLR, Past Life Regression therapy. One of the artists I know from the market was telling me about it. She said she feels so inspired to paint after she's had a session. And I've decided to showcase some of my own work, so I'll take all the inspiration I can get right now. We *have* to go."

"Nat, you are an artistic genius. You're probably the most successful art gallery owner in Illinois, and this just sounds weird. Anyway, I thought you found a new muse? Didn't we *just* finish talking about the rich trophy wife you're hot and heavy with?"

"Yeah, she's great, but ... I thought I would see what this PLR is all about, you know, get some *extra* inspiration." She closes her sentence with a slow, exaggerated wink. "I only have a month before the exhibit. Come on, Jones. You know what they say. *Like the good ole days.* Come to therapy with me."

"Nat, *I am* a therapist! A real therapist, well almost. I didn't spend the last five years studying behavioral therapy to have some voodoo doctor put a spell on me."

"You should have an open mind to other forms of ... perspective, Jones."

As usual, I am the moth to her flame.

"Explain to me what this involves."

She starts gushing immediately. "It's a form of hypnosis. Here, I have the brochure in my purse." She dives into her oversized Fendi tote and begins to rummage through the mess of contents and doesn't stop talking. "The therapist's name is Rachel—Rachel Kimble—Diploma in Regression Therqapy Certified Master Hypnotist all that shit." She's foraging deep into the inner pockets now. "She's just over in Wicker Park. She's some sort of spiritual and—whatcha call it?— metaphysical healer."

Honestly, who needs a purse that big?

"She can read your—here it is!—past life and stuff!" Triumphant, she dangles the crumpled brochure in front of me.

"Go on." I try to hide my amusement behind my hand over my lips.

She reads off the front cover. "'What is Past Life Regression?' Look, each of those letters has a capital. That means it's a serious discipline. 'A personal growth process allowing an individual to bring to consciousness any unresolved issues, past or present, which impacts his or her life. During the process, one will discover what the soul learned long ago, and how the lessons of the past reflect in your life today.' Shut up . . . this sounds amazing!" Natalie squeals. "We are so going to do this."

"Fine, I'll go."

"Really? Yay! We're booked for Thursday."

"Nat!" My voice strains against the words and the resulting screech turns heads in our direction. "That's in two days. Two days! You can't just spring this stuff on me! I need notice. I'm sure Bo has a function for us that night."

For a brief moment, she is wide-eyed with disbelief, then she raises her right hand and flashes me her palm, seamlessly changing to the I-know-you-didn't-just-give-me-attitude look that Nat mastered when she was fifteen years old. "Jeez. Chill, Jones. I'm sure Bo can release you from his talons for a few hours."

"I'm sorry, it's just . . . I have this pounding headache that won't go away." She won't believe me. I know it, even as I say it. I want so badly to talk to her about what's been going on, but she's not really the listening kind. She's more the I'll-fucking-castrate-him kind. I've married the guy my friends would castrate.

□ □ □

It's Thursday afternoon and still raining. I'm staring out the window of my office, following the raindrops with my finger as they hit the glass. It's like watching a game of Plinko on *The Price is Right*. Just when you think you know what path the raindrop is going to take, it changes course. I should be going through my patient files, but I'm absorbed in this magnificent, simple distraction that Mother Nature has conjured for me.

I don't know how long I've been standing there, frozen in time, when my phone goes off.

There's no ignoring it. I'm on call, and I don't want to be responsible for a patient's relapse. "Hello, Izabel Carmichael speaking."

"Sup, bitch?" Natalie has the worst gangster voice I've ever heard.

I sigh. She knows what I'm about to say, and she brushes it off with a laugh.

"Just thought I would brush up on my urban vernacular. Street art is huge right now, so I need to know the lingo."

I sigh again. Sometimes talking to her is like dealing with a toddler who needs direction to maintain focus. "What can I do for you, Nat?"

"Ugh, you know you *are* actually kind of bitchy today. Are you ragging?"

"No. Just busy."

"Listen, Jones, I know I made a big deal about our appointment tonight, but I have to cancel."

"What?" My annoyance with her is at an all-time high, and I can't keep the bite from my tone.

"I know, I know. I'm so bummed, but there's this painting I've been trying to track down for months. I finally located it and met with the supplier last week, but I need to finalize the details tonight to nab it in time for the exhibit. I'll make it up to you, I promise."

"Well, I'm not going if you're not coming with me. This was your idea."

"No, no, no! You have to go! You already changed your schedule around and everything.

I'm doing my meet up at 2Kats, so you come after and tell me all about it over drinks."

"Nat—"

"Really, Jones, you're gonna love it. It's going to be so cool!"

"No! Come on, Nat, this is dumb. We'll reschedule."

"Jones, it's like four p.m. You can't bail on the lady now. That'd be rude." *Checkmate.*

"For a best friend, you're actually the worst sometimes."

"Yeah, but you love me!" She starts making kissing sounds through the phone. "2Kats, eight thirty, see you then." *Click.*

I toss my phone on my desk and smile. She's right, I do love her.

5

Rain or not, alone or with Nat, I do love the Wicker Park neighborhoods. The streets are canopied with zelkova trees. Front lawn gardens are lush and trimmed with stout, wrought iron fencing. I pull up in front of the three-story brownstone a few minutes early.

I send Bo a quick email to remind him I'm meeting up with Natalie later. He was, of course, less than thrilled when I told him about our plans for tonight. Message sent, there's nothing to do but get out of the car and head up the walk.

I'm buzzed in over an intercom into a quiet hallway with ridiculously creaky wood floors. A faint aroma of patchouli lingers in the air. For a moment, I just stand there, trying not to shift my weight and cause more squeaking, trying to steady myself. Suddenly, I'm overcome with nerves.

I knock on door D and am greeted by a lady in her mid-fifties. She looks a little unkempt. Her long, gray, wiry hair is pulled back in a messy French braid, and she is wearing a full-length, flowy skirt and Birkenstocks. I'm not sure why her appearance shocks me. What did I expect her to look like?

"Welcome! You must be Izabel. Please, come in." She moves to the side and ushers me to her living room.

The patchouli smell clearly comes from in here. I scan the room and notice a large Buddha statue in the corner, an icon of the Virgin Mary and Jesus, and a collage of Hindu deities. I wasn't aware one could be so theologically diverse.

"I'm sorry. I seem to have forgotten my manners." I extend my hand to shake hands with her.

"It's a pleasure to meet you, Izabel. I'm Rachel Kimble. Please have a seat and let me know what I can do for you today." Rachel fans her free arm toward the seats on the other side of the room.

"I'm not really sure. My friend Natalie booked this appointment, then she had to cancel at the last minute. I guess I'm here for a Past Life Regression session?"

"Yes, of course. And yet, I must say, you seem dubious. Why is that?"

She's watching me fidget, which only increases my need to squirm. "Like I said, my friend booked this appointment. So, I'm not really sure what to expect or whether I even believe in a past life."

To this, she nods, with the glimmer of a small grin. "Completely understandable. How about I begin by explaining the process to you, and if you'd rather not proceed then we can say our goodbyes? But I have to say, I felt a surge of energy when you first arrived. I think you'll be pleasantly surprised with what you could learn here today."

I remember Natalie's words: *You should have an open mind to other forms of therapy.* "Actually, I'm ready to just get started. I'm ready to try it."

"All right, Izabel. Lean back in the chair and close your eyes. Take a few long, cleansing breaths—in through your nose and out through your mouth. I want you to clear your mind of all distractions. Imagine yourself walking through a beautiful meadow, feel the flowers on your fingers. The sun is shining on your face. Feel the heat blanket your body. Continue to breathe— nice and slow. Now, I'm going to count back from ten and when you reach the end of the meadow you will enter a past life. Ten . . . nine . . . eight . . ."

□ □ □

The Blue Note is a flurry tonight, despite all the raids. Sal and Sammy Giambati seem immune to prohibition. Supplying Detroit's finest with hooch and girls will do that for you, I guess. The band is in full swing. I love when Fat Ray and the boys play.

Josephine is on top of the bar, captivating her audience with flashes of flesh. The men can't take their eyes off her when she performs, and who could blame them? She's a real Sheba. Her fiery red curls fall just below her perfectly round breasts. Her waist is cinched in by a black lace corset. She has the most exquisite lingerie—care of the Giambatis, I suspect. You always deck out your top girl. She exudes sexuality. I must remember to ask what her secret is. I wonder if she's come as long a way as I have. The memory of my first customer makes me blush.

Mama was showing me the ropes. Mama takes care of all the girls in every way, from makeup, to ciggies, to women's needs. I was perched at the bar sipping gin to calm my nerves. I had my dress hiked up high enough to show the skin above my stockings when I crossed my legs, just like Mama told me to do.

The club was buzzing with rowdy soldiers and sailors, but I noticed one bell bottom in particular. He was more reserved than the others, almost shy, and he looked delicious—tall and slim, slicked back dark hair with the dashing good looks of a film star. We locked eyes, so I winked at him and curled my finger for him to come over—again, all Mama's coaching. He couldn't have been any older than me. I was so nervous. I wasn't even sure what I'd do once he reached me. Seconds later, he was standing in front of me, and all I could think to say was, "Butt me."

He took out two cigarettes from his case and lit them both, passing one to me. We stared at each other for a few minutes, wafting in and out of the smoke before I caught Mama's eye from across the room: Go!

My hand fit so well in his. He followed me like a puppy up the stairs to the boudoirs. I closed the door behind us, and before I even finished turning around, he grabbed me awkwardly and slathered wet kisses onto my cheek and neck.

"Slow down, lover." I squirmed out of his grip.

He dropped his head in embarrassment. "I'm sorry." His voice was little more than a pained, embarrassed whisper. "Was I doing it wrong?"

"You've never been with a woman, handsome?"

"No." I wanted to tell him it was my first time too, but Mama said men pay for pleasure, not ignorance.

"Don't worry, doll." I ran a hand down his arm, trying to comfort him. "We'll have fun." I supposed I'd have to make it up. "Lie down on the bed."

I clambered on top of him and started to move my hips. I could feel his manhood growing through his uniform and increased my rhythm, gyrating deeper onto him, then leaned forward to blow into his ear. Suddenly, he grabbed my hips and convulsed under me. Already?

"Was that—"

"I'm sorry."

"Oh . . . We can try again. Your time's not up yet."

After shimmying down his legs, I undid his belt and zipper, and slid his pants off. I laid them flat on the floor so they'd dry out before he went back downstairs. I stood up to remove my panties, then lay down beside him.

"Kneel between my legs."

He obeyed. Who knew I could be a teacher of such intimacies? It was such an electric feeling.

I grabbed his adequate erection and guided him to my wetness. He pushed into me, slowly, my hands on the small of his back. He thrusted, once, twice . . . then groaned and collapsed on top of me. Again!

The applause snaps me out of my daydream. Josephine is dancing completely naked behind two oversized feather fans. She moves the fans with such grace and elegance, never revealing too much. When the song is finished, she turns to face the back wall and drops the fan covering her buttocks. She peeks over her shoulder, winks at her lust-struck men, and rewards them with a wiggle of her exquisite derriere. The men go wild. Our little joint must be heard all the way to Oak Park. *Gosh, she really knows how to work up the crowd.*

"Eve!" Mama snaps her fingers in my face. "You ain't here to watch Josephine. Come on, there's a fella who wants to meet you."

I slide off the bar stool, perk up my breasts, and follow Mama through the crowd. One of the drunken sailors smacks my ass as I pass, and slurs, "Dance for me, sugar."

"Another time, doll." I cast him a bogus smile as I barely manage the words.

Mama stops in front of one of the tables and starts talking to the man sitting down. "This is Eve." She shifts so he can get a better look at me, and I'm greeted by the kindest eyes I have ever seen.

He stands, takes my hand in his, and kisses the tops of my fingers. "It's a pleasure to meet you, Eve. My name is Charlie. Charlie Rudolph."

His stunning good looks have left me speechless. He has mid-length, silky dark hair and a bristly five o'clock shadow, but oh my, those *eyes*—piercing green, warm, so vivid and clear— hint that our meeting was undeniable.

"I would be delighted if you would accompany me upstairs. That is, of course, if this would suit you, Eve?" He grazes his lips across my fingers again. It's like the room and all its people and mayhem is melting away from us and everything comes down to his warm breath on my fingertips, the edge of his teeth as he grazes my knuckles. Never have I wanted a man to make love to me as desperately as I want him at this very moment.

"Eve!" Mama snaps me out of the sensual haze created by his touch. "What are you waiting for? Show the gentleman upstairs."

"Madam, may I have a word with you first?" Charlie gently ushers Mama a few steps from me.

"But of course," Mama coos, clearly smitten with his glaring charm.

When he returns, he offers me his arm. I wrap mine through his and we walk toward the staircase.

"What did you say to Mama?" I haven't been this bashful talking to a man since I don't know when . . . maybe my first john.

"I told her, if it pleases you, I would like for you to remain my companion for the duration of my stay in Detroit."

"What was her answer?"

"I wasn't asking her permission. I'm asking for yours, Eve." He stops and turns so our bodies are flush. "You are the most magnificent creature. I must confess, I'm half-bewitched. Your blush, your smile. Your plump, red lips. You are irresistible. Delectable."

"But . . . you don't even know me." How can I be the subject of this ardent outpouring? He tilts his head down and rests his lips on mine. I close my eyes, and the pulse of our breathing becomes one.

"I've watched you. You are the one I've been waiting for." He cradles my head in his hands, and before I can reply, he kisses me tenderly. Then he slowly releases me from his caress, tugging gently on my bottom lip. "Say yes," he whispers onto my lips.

"Yes!" Yes . . . *I would be yours forever.*

6

Josephine brushes out my hair in long strokes down my back. We sit in front of the oversized vanity. Her room is adorned with extravagances—feathers and pearls and paintings, each a gift from another smitten lover. A soft piano melody plays in the background from her gramophone. She told me the name of the composer, but I don't remember. All I know is he's French, and it has something to do with the moon. It makes me happy just to hear it.

Without fail, a man proposes to Josephine before the sun rises each day. And every time, she finds a gracious new way to decline. She could be a rich man's wife—go anywhere, see anything, travel the country where that beautiful music comes from—but she loves what she does. She's an empress, and her kingdom is built on men.

All I know is, if my gentleman walked in tonight and asked me to run away with him, I wouldn't even pause to pack a bag.

My Charlie Rudolph is indeed a gentleman of the highest class. I'm not just a harlot to him. With Charlie

I'm . . . I'm important. He's been studying something called Buddhism, and according to the Dalai Lama, he and I will spend many lifetimes together. I'm not sure what that means, or who this Lama guy is, but even to have one life with Charlie would be enough.

"Your hair is so beautiful, Eve. You should leave it down tonight." Josephine rests the brush on her vanity next to her European face cream and walks to her closet. "Wear this, and your Mr. Rudolph will never let you go." She hands me a long, cream-colored silk gown that looks very expensive. "Put it on, doll. You'll look fabulous in it."

"I couldn't. It must have cost you a month's pay."

"Nah, my Friday guy brought this back for me after his last trip to Paris. I want you to wear it. Besides, it'll make your breasts look divine." She winks at me and pokes just the tip of her tongue in between her lips.

I slide off my dressing robe and step into the gown. The luxurious material glides up my body like cool, sudsy water. The fit is snug, but Josephine is right. The fabric clings to my breasts like a glove to fingers. There is a slit up the side exposing one of my long legs. The front of the gown is a deep V and the back scoops all the way down to the top of my behind. It feels so delicately smooth against my skin.

I admire my reflection for a brief moment. This is what grandeur feels like. I see Josephine behind me, beaming with her own adoration. She steps closer and drapes a string of pearls around my neck so they hang down my back.

"You look stunning. Your Mr. Rudolph will be left speechless. *Entre deux coeurs qui s'aiment, nul besoin de paroles.* Two hearts in love need no words," she translates. "There is one final step to complete." Josephine turns me away from the mirror to face her. Delicately, like an artist, she applies vivid red lipstick, smooth as satin, to my puckered lips, smudging the edge with her pinkie.

"Mmm. It tastes like cherry."

"Just one last thing." She bends her head and kisses me—a long, deep river of a kiss, where she is the stream and I am the riverbed. I am no puritan, but I have never kissed a woman before. I can't move, but all the while my abdomen clenches and unclenches, and something I don't know within myself wants to savor the taste of her tongue.

"I see why he finds your lips so irresistible, Eve. I have to go downstairs now. Shut my door when you leave. Don't be long. I'm sure he's waiting for you." She slips away, leaving me to my lust. I need to find Charlie to fill this wanting.

It's all I can do not to run into the hallway. At the banister overlooking the club, I perch my hand on the rail and cock my hip. I am a wanton goddess in this moment, roiling with desire. Scanning the room, I see him looking up at me, his chair turned away from the stage. He rises and makes his way to the stairs, never breaking our gaze. With every step he takes, my fever rises. He moves sleek and slow like a panther as he ascends closer to me, making love to me with his eyes, with every bewitching step he takes.

It's as if the sound of his heels on the steps matches my heartbeat—heavy and steady.

After what seems like an eternity, we stand flush to one another.

"You are breathtaking, Eve. I have never seen a more beautiful woman."

I bashfully look down at the ground. The heat from my blush tells me my cheeks are glowing crimson red.

He lifts my chin to look at him. "Don't ever doubt. It's true. You are luminous this evening and always."

"Thank you, Charlie." Looking deep into his eyes, I am stricken by his sincerity.

"Let me escort you to your room. I don't want an audience for this."

He leads me back down the hall, tosses his satchel by the door, and lifts me into an embrace. He is a Goliath against my curvy frame. I slide back down his taut body, my feet grazing the floor. He spins me and admires the gown as it pulls against my flesh. With one feather-light finger he draws a straight line down my exposed back from my neck to my rear.

"How is it possible that you're even more beautiful in this gown? Although nothing can compare to..." He trails off, but I take his meaning from his devilish grin.

Charlie hooks his fingers under the straps of my gown and inches the material away from my shoulders, down my arms, past my breasts, halting at my waist. He devotes a kiss to the top of each breast and releases the gown from his fingers. The silk trickles away, sending waves of pleasure back up between my legs.

He moans at the sight of me and pulls me into a gentle embrace, buries his face into my neck, and inhales deeply. "You smell divine. Lie on the bed. I want to do something that I think you will enjoy."

Intrigued, excited, aroused, I do as I am bid and prop up on my elbows so I can watch his every move.

He removes his suit jacket and folds it over the back of the chair, then slowly pulls down his suspenders and lets them hang below his waist.

"Are you strip teasing me, Mr. Rudolph?" I feel the heat return, but this time it's driven by desire.

He winks, then, much to my satisfaction, removes his crisp, white collar shirt and tosses it to me—a move I have performed for him on many occasions since we met. I grab hold of it and lift it to my nose, inhaling his scent, branding it into my soul: musk oil and vanilla tobacco mixed with his sweet perspiration. He unfolds his art satchel and takes out a long paintbrush with a feathered, fanned tip.

The anticipation is eating away at me. "Am I to watch you paint?"

"Something like that." He unhooks his belt and his pants drop to the floor.

He pins me, pushing me flat onto the mattress with the heft of his body. I can feel every hard inch of him pressing into me. He's so close, close to where I want him. My hips are rising, pushing against him, trying to rub against that warm, rigid member.

"Close your eyes. Be a good girl and don't open them."

I obey. There's nothing to be done about it. I am his slave. Adrenaline rushes through me again as I wait for his first touch, waiting for him to plunge inside me. Tin and glass chinking.

What is he going to do to me? Cold liquid spreads down my throat and collarbone. I gasp. With a plodding pace, he moves the brush toward my chest and paints little circles around my erect nipples. My breathing accelerates and I arch my back, lifting my breasts closer to him.

"*Please.*" The word escapes as half-breath, half-moan. I'm fumbling for his erection, trying to get it between my fingers.

Charlie says nothing but continues to cascade the brush down the center line of my belly and circles around my naval. I feel his body slide down my legs and the brush follows in an S pattern across my thighs to my knees.

"Charlie. Please, I want you inside me." I can't hide the desperation in my voice.

He remains silent, but leans into me, pressing himself into my thigh. I am hot, dripping turmoil.

The brush crawls down my shins until I feel it at my feet. I shiver at the sensation. He weaves the bristles between my toes. I tremble and squeeze my legs together at the knees, craving pressure there, craving fullness. The paint on the rest of my body has tightened every pore on my skin and is starting to crack.

"Charlie!" I have reached my brim. I need his touch, his flesh to mine.

Before I know it, he is in me. I release a thankful, most unladylike groan. My hips automatically move to his rhythm, his cock filling me with every thrust. If he could just stay inside me forever, just deeper and deeper . . .

He slows his pace and kisses me tenderly. "I want to cherish every moment with you, Eve. I love you."

I wrap my arms and legs around him and fall into the hypnotic cadence of Charlie Rudolph. I don't want him to find his release; I will always want more. This is where we belong—at the place where he and I do not exist, only *we*. After losing ourselves for what seems like hours, we quietly shatter around each other. With one fluid motion, he rolls over on the bed so that I am perched above him.

"What are you grinning about?" I brush sweat from his brow.

After a long, content sigh, he responds. "You are like a little feather from an angel's wing that has just landed on me from the heavens. I like when you are on me. You warm me to the core." He wraps his arms around me and pulls me into an embrace. "I wish we were the last two people on earth and were responsible for starting the human race over. There would be no war or poverty and all the girls would have your beauty and tenacity—"

I interrupt. "And all the boys would be as smart"—I kiss one eyelid—"and as kind"—I kiss his other eyelid—"and as handsome as you." I kiss the tip of his nose.

His grin slips into a frown. "Eve, I have some good news and bad news for you. Which should I tell you first?"

"Bad." I say it as more of a question than an answer.

"All right. I have to go back to New York tomorrow. I have some family business to deal with, that frankly I have been avoiding for a while now."

I give Charlie an exaggerated pout and stick out my bottom lip. He grabs it between his teeth and tugs me in for a kiss.

"The good news is I have made arrangements with Mama to spend the entire night with you."

My eyes widen and I squeal with excitement. I wiggle on top of him and immediately feel his own growing excitement. He gives my rump a smack.

"Tsk-tsk, missy. I will not let you distract me. Up you go. I have some painting to do."

He flips me back so I am underneath him again and slides off my body toward the end of the bed, but not before stopping and bestowing a taunting kiss on my sex, making me bow off the bed.

Licking his lips, he smiles up at me. "Mmm, I will continue this later."

7

It's Saturday night and the crowd is buzzing around the joint. The fog of cigarette smoke wafts through the dim light around the room. Josephine is on her usual perch, doing what she does best. I'm at the bar, sipping gin to calm my nerves.

I'm especially anxious tonight because I get to see him again—the artist, my artist. I've been waiting two long days for this night, rushing through my last few johns in fear that my Charlie would leave the club if he didn't see me. I wanted to turn down every man that approached me these last couple of days, but Mama and the brothers would never allow that.

After all, I'm here to service these men. Having sex with no strings, no attachment, then gladly tucking a cash tip into my garter once we're finished has never been an issue . . . that is, until I laid eyes on him, *my Charlie*. Now he is all I think about.

I receive no pleasure being with other men. One time, I even yawned mid-thrust. I had to pinch myself to stay awake. Their hands pawing at me might as well be talons scratching at my skin. Tonight, after almost pushing the last John, Bob, or Ted, or whatever his name was, out of my room, I washed up as quickly as possible to look fresh and pretty for Charlie. I'm wearing my black- and cream-colored knee-length silk kimono robe, which I've tied loosely to reveal the inside rounds of my breasts, and my garter is high up my thigh to hold my ciggies.

My stomach churns as I scan the room for him. He is the most incredible—*the only*— lover I've ever had, but it's more with Charlie. He asks permission of me. We talk for hours about everything from Darwin to Dickens to the Industrial Revolution, and all the while, he paints my portrait, paints what he calls my post-coital luminescence. Well, he talks, and I lap it up. I asked him once why he spends all of his time with a plain Jane like me and not someone more glamorous like Josephine.

Without a second thought he replied, "You, Eve . . ." He paused, his luminous green eyes penetrating mine with longing, "Are my muse. When I look at you, my brush just moves. You are perfection!"

Gino, the doorman, swings the door wide for a familiar face. There he is. My heart flutters. Ushered to a vacant table, he hands the bellboy his art case to take upstairs, and already a flock of girls swoop in. I can't blame them. He has rugged good looks and those eyes . . . those beautiful green eyes, they're . . . they're mesmerizing. "Sammy, grab me a whiskey, will ya?"

"Sure thing, doll."

I can luxuriate for a little moment as the whiskey pours. He's looking for me, and there's something wonderfully intoxicating about that look.

He's too much of a gentleman to tell the ladies he's not interested. I take my cue to rescue him. With whiskey in hand, I strut confidently toward his table. The girls know to scram when I get there. You don't interfere with someone's regular.

I slip lightly onto his lap and instantly feel his excitement through the cool silk of my robe. I grin. He missed me as well. I place the whiskey on the table and take out the ciggie case I have stashed in my garter. I roll a cigarette between my thumb and pointer finger, lick the tip, and pucker it between my lips, my eyes never leaving his. He pulls a light from his pocket and flicks off a flame. I lean into it and take a long drag before offering it to his lips. We smoke in silence for a minute or two until he throws his whiskey back and stands, gently placing me on my feet. My knees wobble. The excitement of knowing what is about to happen builds. He tilts his head toward the stairs and flashes a lascivious smile.

I want him to take me right now on this table. We dash to our room and kick the door closed. I untie the loose belt around my waist and let the robe slide to the floor. It sends chills through my over-sensitized body, and my nipples harden. He inhales sharply, and I see the appreciation in his eyes. Even though he knows every inch of my body now, I always feel stunning in his eyes.

He closes the distance between us and wraps his arms around me. I sink into his tender embrace. He plants a tender kiss in the depression above my clavicle and accepts my faint moan as permission to lay me on the bed, and thus begins his routine. Starting at my forehead, he slowly kisses his way down my body.

"You"—he says between heavy breaths—"are my canvas." He stops over my nipples, teasing one then the other with his teeth ever so gently. "I"—he plants a kiss in between my ribs—"am the brush."

I'm writhing, my legs spread wide, my hips flexing upward. He pauses over my pubic hair and breathes in heavily. "And this"—exhale—"is my masterpiece." Then he unleashes his tongue on me.

I grab his head with my hands and wrap my legs around his shoulders, pushing his face into me. Twirling in little circles, his expert tongue laps at me steadily. Oh, how is it possible that this feels better than last time? I'm so close already, and my fingers clench his hair. It's building and building . . . and with one final flick, I begin to convulse, my body no longer my own. I fall flat, completely satisfied, entirely unwound, and he rests between my legs for a few minutes with his head on my belly as I twist his hair between my fingers.

"How did I manage to stay away from you for two days?" He kisses up my body until he is lying next to me.

"Well, I didn't miss you one bit," I tease him while undoing the top button of his pants to give his throbbing manhood a generous squeeze. With that, he pounces and slowly eases into me.

"Mmm. I have missed your cock though."

I sit on the edge of the chair, stretching slightly forward to fiddle with the pearls around my neck. The last time I wore them, he worked the string into his painting. He says they elongate my already beautiful back. I tried to return them to Josephine, but she wouldn't have it. She told me it brings her joy to see me wear them.

I borrowed her gramophone as well. Charlie enjoys listening to music while he paints. The moon song—"Clair de Lune," Charlie taught me—plays in the background. Half the time when Charlie schools me, I can hardly remember what he said to me the next day. I just love listening to him speak. His voice is hypnotizing and soothing, and he explains everything with such humility and patience.

"Stop fidgeting, please."

"When can I see?"

"When the time is right, my love. Now, sit still. I'm nearly finished."

I straighten myself and pull my shoulders back to the pose. Staring over my shoulder at Charlie, I study the lines of his face. He looks so serious when he paints, but ever just as lovely.

"Are you sleepy?"

I nod, and he holds out his hands, inviting me over to him. I leap from my chair and crawl into his lap, nestling my head onto his chest, and close my weary eyes. Charlie hugs me in closer under the nook of his arm.

"What are you going to do with it when you've finished?" I manage to ask the question before I am unable to stifle a yawn.

"I'm going to hang it on my wall so I can look at you whenever my heart desires."

Deep down, his answer saddens me. I want it to be

that he will hang it in the study of the home we will share back in New York, that the reason he left for those two days was to get everything ready for my arrival.

I can picture our house now. Through the front entrance, there's an extravagant staircase that winds up both sides of the walls that meet at a landing. A huge, crystal chandelier hangs above the great room, which extends all the way to the back of the house, to the glass doors that lead out to the terrace overlooking our garden. Floor-to-ceiling windows let in the sunlight, and big, plush, upholstered furniture sits in every room, even the kitchen, where I cook all of our meals, every day.

And children! We would have so many children. Their voices and giggles would travel throughout the entire house like cherubs playing their harps. And at the end of the day, after I have tucked all of the children into their beds and kissed them all good night, I would lay my head down beside my darling Charlie and melt into a peaceful slumber.

My eyes flutter open to the soft flicker of light that fills the room. I'm jubilant by the most glorious dream I was having. When I look around, Charlie is up and dressed. All of his art supplies are packed away, and he is buckling up his satchel.

"Come back to bed," I squeak and stretch my arms over my head.

He saunters over to the bed and sits next to me. He locks his eyes on mine, and then trails kisses down my face, stopping on my lips. "I have to go, my love."

"Nooo!"

He stands and picks up his bag.

Urgently, I sit up. "But you didn't even show me the painting. Wait!"

"You'll see it one day, my darling." He offers me a weak smile and opens the door, but he pauses to look back at me. "I love you. Forever, Eve." Then he's gone.

8

"And . . . Welcome back, Izabel. How do you feel?" Rachel asks.

The dull rays of the setting sun reflect off the metal dream catcher hanging in front of the window. The light catches my eye, jolting me out of my haze.

"How long was I out? It feels like . . . a lifetime."

"You were under for ninety minutes. It was quite an intense session. How do you feel?"

I take a long, deep breath through my nose and hold it for a second or two before exhaling through my mouth. "Uneasy. Like something is missing. It felt so *real*. Like I was there. My brain's on overdrive."

Rachel nods. "Well, in some capacity you *were* there. This is your story, Izabel. You will experience as much, or as little, as your subconscious will convey. Metaphysically, your visions and perceptions are endless. You have to embrace the immeasurable possibilities of your mind's aptitude."

I stare at her as though I don't understand English. "This is . . . a lot to absorb."

"You are absolutely correct. Most people leave their

first PLR session feeling a little apprehensive. Don't overthink it. Just enjoy what you've experienced and take any knowledge you've brought back with you as enlightenment."

I have no intelligible response for her. I just sit there wide-eyed, my mouth half open. "Do you have any questions for me, Izabel?"

The glint of light from the dream catcher distracts me. Taunting me to go back—back to him. I want—I *need* to go back. Why did he leave?

"Izabel?" I hear the soft voice again.

I have a million questions, I want to shout. "No. Not that I can think of right now."

"Well then, it seems our time together has ended for now. Feel free to contact me if you have any questions or would like to book another session." Rachel walks me to the door, turns to me, and bows. "Sending you light and love, Izabel. Namaste."

I mimic her motion then step into the hallway. I stand immobile for a few minutes, gathering my thoughts. *Don't overthink this, Izabel.*

Yeah, right.

□ □ □

I pull up to the valet in front of the Emily Hotel around 8:20 p.m. 2Kats is on the twenty- first floor, overlooking the lake, and according to Natalie, it's the bar *du jour*. I don't even remember the drive here. *Did I obey the street signs?*

I hand the valet attendant my keys and stagger into the lobby. There seems to be a lot of commotion going on that I'm not prepared for. The lobby bar is packed with men donning the after-hours business suit look—no tie and top two buttons undone. There is a man arguing with one of the front desk clerks about his reservation mix up. Two kids whip past me yelling, "You're it!"

It's all so normal, but my skin is crawling. I can't make it into the elevator fast enough. The doors close, and I roll my eyes upward and exhale, silently thanking whoever's up there that I don't have to ride up with anyone else. The *ding* at the twenty-first floor makes me jump.

Seriously, Izabel, what is wrong with you?

Even this bar is just so *busy*. I walk farther into the tight-knit crowd, and I hear her before I see her—Natalie, glowing and in her element. She is like the Pied Piper, and beautiful people flock to her. When she spots me, she dismisses her minions, skips over, and throws her arms around me, giving me an extra-amorous Natalie hug.

"Happy to see me, Nat?"

She releases me to arm's length and gives me the once-over. "What's wrong? Are you mad at me for canceling?" Her eyes narrow. "Did something happen at the session?"

Of course, not even a pumping techno beat, hordes of people, and strobe lighting could throw her off. Like a lion on a gazelle, she's got me.

"Come on, Nat, let's get a glass of wine and I'll tell you all about it. On second thought, let's make it a bottle. I don't have clinic tomorrow."

"That's my girl." Natalie grabs my face between her

hands and plants an unchaste kiss on my lips. When she lets go, we notice three overzealous men ogling us. "What are you douchebags looking at?" she snarls at them.

They retreat straight away, and I almost feel bad for them.

"Come on." Natalie grabs my hand and leads me toward a table in the back corner. "Let's get that wine."

We're on our second bottle because of Nat's two-glasses-to-my-one pace, and she hasn't uttered a single word. I must remember to mark this moment down somewhere because nobody will ever believe me. I've talked well into the night about my PLR experience, about the club, and Mama, and how Josephine totally reminded me of her. I tell her about Eve and Charlie and how much they loved each other despite how different their lives were.

I pause for a minute to reflect and take a sip of my wine. And then I see the reflection of a man I recognize in the mirror behind Natalie. Cold electricity flashes across my body.

"Jones, what happened? You look like you're gonna hurl."

I close my eyes and shake my head. "It's nothing. I thought I saw someone I know. Maybe the wine is getting to me a little . . . Anyway, enough about my appointment. Tell me how the gallery show is coming along."

That's all it takes to get Natalie off my trail. She starts into a diatribe about useless assistants and customs brokers who have no clue how valuable these items are. She tells me about her trophy wife and their earlier rendezvous here in the bathroom stall—how she made her orgasm three times in a row. Incidentally, she couldn't stay to meet me; she had family commitments.

Nat is making me laugh though, in her crude Natalie way, and I really am having a good time. I miss our all-nighters.

"Holy shit, what time is it?" I panic, and for a moment, her expression mirrors the emotion surging through me.

She checks her phone. "It's almost twelve thirty. Are you going to get an earful from Bo?"

I'm sure it'll be more than that. I give her a weak smile. "No, he'll be fine."

As I walk to my car, I quickly do a mental calculation of drinks per hour in my head.

Three and a half hours, three glasses of wine, and two glasses of soda water. I'll be okay. I take my phone out to call Bo and let him know I'm on my way. I decide to send him a text instead in case he's sleeping. He doesn't sleep well on the best of nights, and I'd hate to wake him. If he is asleep, he won't know I got home a little late. I continue my chant, *he won't know*, the entire drive home.

I tiptoe into the house at exactly one a.m. It's quiet and dark except for the glow of the range light in the kitchen. I gently place my purse on the floor, the clink from the chain-link strap echoing down the hall. *Shit! Shhh!* My anxiety is at an all-time high, and I'm not sure which Bo I'll be greeted with. I make my way into the kitchen for some water before I go to bed. When I walk through the door, I see him sitting on the counter. "Where the fuck have you been?"

I'm galvanized with fear, trying to answer him, but my brain refuses to communicate with my mouth.

"Answer me!" he shouts.

"I . . . I was out with Natalie. I sent you an email earlier today reminding you. Didn't you get it?"

He shakes his head.

"Bo, please, we don't have to fight about this." I need to calm him down before this gets out of control.

You can do this. Remember: calm, non-defensive, and respectful reaction. My email comment probably didn't help. But what was I supposed to say?

He hops off the counter and walks toward me. Instinctively, I start to back away. "Bo, this is a simple case of miscommunication. Let's sit down and talk about what is making you so angry. I apologize for being late. Next time . . . next time I'll . . . I will be more considerate. I'll call you instead of relying on email."

"Next time . . ." He grabs his hair between his fingers and growls, "For Christ's sake, don't psychoanalyze me. Do you fucking enjoy making me angry?"

"Let's talk about this in the dining room." I turn to leave the kitchen, but he grabs my arm before I can get away.

He pulls me so hard, I hit my head on the cabinet and collapse to the ground. I curl myself into a protective ball on the floor, but the next blow doesn't come. Instead, he drops down beside me and pulls me into his lap. I'm too afraid of what he'll do if I pull away, so I let him. He strokes my hair and rocks me back and forth.

"I'm so sorry, baby. I didn't mean to do that. What have I done?" The unbearable mantra begins. We sit on the floor for what seems like hours. He apologizes, he grieves, he weeps. I listen. If promises made on the kitchen floor were kept, he'd never hit me again.

□ □ □

When I wake, I'm in our bed alone, still dressed in last night's clothes. Bo must have carried me in after I fell asleep in his lap. I survey the room. The blinds are drawn, but a sliver of light shines through, so I know it must be morning.

I roll onto my side and the pain in my head rushes in. I notice a large bouquet of flowers, a Tiffany box, and a note on the bedside table. When did he have time to do all this? I glance at the clock. *Holy crap. It's two p.m.* My body defies my attempt to jump out of bed. I sit up slowly and grab the note and the box. I unfold the note.

I'm sorry. I love you.

Is he in the house? I don't think I could face him right now. The white silk ribbon falls effortlessly down the side of the box despite my shaking hands. Inside is a blinding, cushion-cut, yellow diamond ring, with a platinum band encrusted with diamonds.

I almost drop the box from my surprise. It's stunning! What kind of message does it send if I accept this? And if I don't? What will happen then? I put the note in the box and place it under my pillow, out of sight.

I need something—something to kill all the hours left in today. Kickboxing should do the trick. I'll text my trainer to see what time he has available. Ignoring my headache, I get out of bed and fetch my purse that's slumped at the front door. I have eight text messages, no doubt all from Nat. I hate lying to her, but it's much easier to do by text. I read as I make my way back to the bedroom.

Did u get home ok?

Hey. How did last night go? Where are u? Let's meet for lunch.

It's noon, what's going on? Are you ok? WTF! Call me ASAP!

I reply to her last text.

Hi. All's good. Can't meet today. Going to the gym. Will call you later. xo

That should buy me a bit of time until I get my thoughts sorted out. There's one last text . . . from Bo.

Hi, baby. Dad called me to go out of town again. I'll be back Sunday. Hope you liked your gift :) Love you!

I look at my phone and silently scream. Clutching it in my fist, I contemplate throwing it against the wall, just for the satisfaction of watching it smash into pieces.

That's my answer! I tighten my grip around the phone, then bring my hands down to my sides and breathe deep, hoping to achieve some serenity.

I furiously begin to compose a text.

Hi, Allen! It's Izabel. Got time for me today around 4 p.m.? KICKBOXING!

I gingerly place the phone on the bedside table. *Poor phone. It's not your fault.*

I walk over to the window and open the blinds to let in some much-needed sunshine.

Memories from the day we moved in replay before me as I look down into the front yard. I can see our boxes, the truck, our snowball fight. That was almost three years ago. We would have been married by then, but Bo's father kept changing the date. Our life was much simpler then.

And Bo was a much happier person. We were both happier.

Once, he blindfolded me and surprised me with a picnic—right there in the front yard. He raked up the leaves into big piles under the tree and covered them with a quilt. We sat out there for hours drinking wine and talking. He talked about being a father, how he wanted a better relationship with his kids—our kids—than he had with his dad. There was never a topic off limits. He wanted my input on everything. How could we let everything get so derailed?

9

I'm standing in line at my favorite coffee bar in Roscoe Village, waiting for my latte, lost in replays of Thursday night. Kickboxing with Allen on Friday was a very temporary fix.

How many times am I going to let Bo promise he will never do it again? It can't always really be my fault.

I specialize in conflict resolution. I have a master's in behavioral psychology! I graduated top of my class. Where are the answers?

It all comes down to Jack Carmichael. *Cold as can be, except when the damn cameras are around. Then you slap on your forged smile and act like you're posing for a Norman Rockwell painting.*

Nothing like an absentee, workaholic dad with his fair share of clandestine "friendships" on the side—Bo knows it, I know it—to royally fuck up a boy. And his mom! She just drowns it all in charity work and Chardonnay. I could analyze this for years.

Jesus, Izzy . . . stop. Stop making excuses for him!

It's exactly what I'd advise a patient. I should practice what I preach. For four years, the psych profs were constantly recommending that students visit a therapist from time to time to better understand the patient's vulnerability and perspective.

Maybe I should talk to Natalie, but she is a grenade at the best of times. Telling her about this would be like pulling out the pin. And if I talk to my mom, she will just find a way to defend him. Last time I tried to talk to her about Bo's less-than-amorous display of affection for me, her only advice was, "Some men have different ways of blowing off steam, darling. Just do your best to keep him happy and everything will be fine." I know Mom means well—she just wants me to have a better life than she had—but at what cost?

"Non-fat latte? Non-fat latte! NON-FAT—"

"Oh! Here!"

The barista glares at me. I grab a lid and a couple of napkins and spin to walk out as fast as I can. I slam up against what feels like a brick wall, but clearly it's the person standing a little too close behind me in the pick-up line. *Seriously, does anyone have any regard for personal space anymore?* I spilled my latte down the front of my dark-blue denim tunic.

"Shit!" I vigorously wipe the front of my dress, my cheeks scorching with equal embarrassment and irritation. "I'm so sorry! I hope I didn't get any on you."

I feel a gentle hand on my wrist, but the shock of it emanates through my body like lightning. When I look up, it's into a pair of the most *familiar* green eyes. *Holy fuck!*

"You're him." The muttered words fall out of my mouth before I can stop myself.

His face caves in on itself a little. Thin crow's feet form in the corners of those striking eyes. "I'm sorry?"

I straighten my stance and clear my throat. "No, I'm so sorry. Please, let me give you money for dry-cleaning. I should pay more attention."

My stranger gives me an amused smile. "It's not necessary, really. It's just a spot."

I have to say something to him. Will he think I'm crazy? Of course, he will. *Here I go.* I take a deep breath. "This is going to sound beyond bizarre but—" I'm interrupted by the leggy blonde who sidles up beside him.

"Ready to go?" She wraps her arm through his.

"Yeah, sure," he replies. He regards me sympathetically. "You all right?"

I look down at the ground, hoping it will open up and swallow me whole. "Yes. Again, I'm sorry."

"Okay then. Well, bye."

I grab the bridge of my nose and squeeze. It feels like a Mack Truck hit me. *What just happened? Who was that guy? It couldn't possibly be him.*

I practically collapse into one of the plush chairs by the exit and fish into my purse for my phone. I can't process any of my thoughts. *What am I doing? Who should I call?* I scroll through my contacts and press *call*. I sit, holding my breath, waiting for an answer on the other end.

"Pick up . . . pick up. Why won't she pick up?"

Click. "You have reached the office of Rachel Kimble. Your call is very important to me. Please leave a detailed message, and I will return your call as soon as possible. Light and love. Namaste."

"H-Hi, um, Rachel, this is Izabel Carmichael. I came to see you last Thursday. I would like to book another appointment with you today. Wait, it's Sunday. Maybe tomorrow then? Please call me." I rattle off my cell phone number, then say, "Thanks. Bye. Did I mention this is Izabel Carmichael? Okay. Bye."

I need to talk to somebody, or my head is going to explode. Natalie's cell goes straight to voice mail too. *What the hell! This can't be happening.*

"Hey, Nat, it's me. Call me as soon as you can. Nothing is wrong. I just need to tell you something. So, call me. Soon!"

I tap my fingers on the armrest, contemplating my next move. Maybe a quick chat with my mother will help. A little dose of reality always does the trick. I dial her number, and she answers on the second ring. Relief floods over me.

"Hello?"

"Hi, Mom."

"Izabel, it's so nice to hear your voice. Everything okay, my love?"

"Yes, I just wanted to say hi. I don't call you enough. How are you?"

"I'm a little tired, darling. I've been working double shifts lately."

"Mom, I've told you that you don't need to work anymore. I can take care of you."

She laughs. "Oh, darling, I wanted you to marry up so you wouldn't have to worry about money, not so you could take care of me. I'll be just fine. Besides, what would I do all day?"

"Why don't you come visit for a few days, Mom? We could go to the spa for some pampering. I'll send the car service."

When I moved out of the house to go to UChicago, Mom decided to downgrade. She said having too much space would make her feel lonely. Always a slice of Catholic guilt with everything she says, my mom. She sold the house I grew up in and moved north of Milwaukee to a quaint, unassuming town on Lake Michigan. She's happy there, although she would never admit it, even if I don't visit as much as she'd like.

"That sounds lovely. Let me see if I can get the time off work. I'll let you know."

"Okay, please try. I could really use some mom time." I am fighting back a sob.

She's silent for a moment, and when she replies I hear the pain and concern in her voice. "Izabel, you know you can come home whenever . . . whenever you need to."

Her loving offer is too much to process, and the lump at the back of my throat swells. *Oh, Mommy, what am I going to do? I'm so confused.* I have to hang up before the tears start to fall.

"I know, Mom. Thank you. I'd better go. We'll talk soon."

"Goodbye, darling girl."

I press *end* and hold the phone to my heart. It pings with a missed call. From Rachel Kimble. *Dammit!*

I bypass the message and call her back immediately. "Hello, Izabel," a pleasant voice answers on the other end.

"Um, hi. How did you know it was me?"

"The gods told me."

"Oh."

She giggles. "No, dear, I have call display. Just a little psychic joke."

"Oh, of course." *Really? We're making jokes now?*

"You seemed anxious when you left your message. I can see you after my last appointment tomorrow at seven p.m. Will that work?"

"Yes, that's perfect. It's been ... a really strange day. I have a couple of questions for you."

"I look forward to seeing you tomorrow then. Light and love, Izabel. Namaste."

"Thank you. Bye."

Just as I press *end,* my phone rings again. Nat's name pops up on my screen. I'll entertain my chat with her another time.

□ □ □

The patchouli doesn't offend as much this time as I walk down Rachel's creaky hallway.

The day's been a wash. I couldn't concentrate on anything. Everything's a thick stew of memories, bruises, love, questions, pain, paint on a girl's thighs, fists, French music, blood, and piercing green, green eyes.

I knock lightly and I'm greeted almost immediately by Rachel's bountiful smile. Her gray mane is loose today and she's wearing glasses. I hadn't noticed last time, but she is quite attractive in a non-traditional sense. Her skin looks so youthful, and she has impeccable posture.

"Izabel, so nice to see you again. Please come in and make yourself comfortable."

In a few big strides, I hurry across the room and drop into the same springback chair as last session. I lean forward and cross my arms around my chest, waiting for Rachel.

Moving like a butterfly against a strong breeze, she slowly flits toward a perch. She sits down gently, her face kind and curious. "Has something happened since we last met? Your energy has altered."

"Something did happen. Some questions have come up since I left on Thursday . . ." I look down at the knots in the floorboards. The silence stretches between us.

"This is your time, Izabel. Take as long as you need."

"My first session was so . . . intense. It was beyond intense, it was transcendent. I want to go back. I made a connection there. A connection I can still feel."

She gives me a soothing smile. "I can guide you through the same path and process we took last time, but it doesn't guarantee the same destination. The universe gave you that connection. Accept the message you received and allow it to cultivate your mind. Free the insecurities you hold onto. The past is a wonderful place to visit, but it does not define who you are in your physical life."

"But can you meet a person in this physical life that you knew from a previous one?"

"Theoretically, yes, but it is very circumstantial. Past life and physical life can cross paths in a myriad of ways. For example, your bank teller could smile at you one day, or you could accidentally bump into someone walking down the sidewalk. These instances may trigger familiarities in your brain. And yes, those people may have had some significance in a past life, whether it was for a nanosecond or for an entire life."

I understand what she's trying to tell me, but it doesn't help. I need to go back and find out what happened with Charlie and Eve. I need to find out who the man in the coffee shop is.

"Izabel, instead of regression, I'd like to take you through a series of breathing exercises that I think may help you feel more . . . settled."

"No. I would like the regression," I snap unintentionally.

Rachel doesn't seem offended, though. She maintains her gentle, soothing smile. "All right. Let's follow the same process as your last visit. Lean back and relax. Uncross your arms and legs." Rachel leans forward and passes me a tissue. I cock my head questioningly. "It's for your gum. You need to be completely relaxed."

"Oh." I hand Rachel the crumpled tissue then sink back into the chair and close my eyes.

"Okay, now imagine the meadow. Walk slowly through the long blades of grass. Skim your fingers across the tips. Count back from ten."

□ □ □

The joint is dark and the music on the record player skips. There are a few sailors passed out on the bar. I'm not far behind. Whiskey is my drink of choice these days, and I've already polished off a half-bottle. Alone. I don't get on much with any of the new girls. Ever since Josephine up and married one of her suitors, it just hasn't been the same.

Out of the corner of my eye, I see the door of the club open. I spin my body around to see who it is. The world spins with me. I'm struck with disappointment again. It's not him. Three hundred eighty days . . . three hundred eighty-one? I lost count. He never came back for me.

"Eve!" Mama Two shouts. Mama—the real one—left as well. She said she didn't like the direction the joint was heading. I should've taken a hint then and left with her.

All Mama Two does is yell and scold and shake her little velvet purse. It's all about the money with her. Louise takes it in the ass, a dollar in her pouch. He gets off jerking it on my face, another buck and a half in that stupid velvet purse.

"Eve!" Her screech is accompanied by a wrenching of her arm for me to come stand beside her.

I stumble off my bar stool, traipsing and tripping toward her blurry image.

"Take this gentleman"—she snickers—"upstairs. He's paid up for an hour."

I give her a soldier's salute, and she walks away. I look over at this so-called gentleman. He's fat and sweaty. His shirt is unbuttoned real low, exposing all the gray and black hairs on his chest. He keeps wiping his forehead with a white handkerchief. What a perfect end to the night.

I sigh and take his hand. "Let's go."

No sooner is the door closed than I'm wrapped in an octopus clench. His hands are all over me. He begins licking my face and neck. The smells of liquor and body odor are revolting. His breaths are stunted and wheezy.

I pull my face away, trying to get some distance between me and his foul, filthy tongue.

Anchoring my hands on his chest, I push with all my might, but he tightens his hold on me. I have to change my tactic here. This will end badly for me if I don't calm him down. I unwillingly stop my struggle and begin to kiss his salty neck. He loosens his grip on me. *Okay, this seems to be working.*

"Come on, Big Daddy. Let's get on the bed so I can take care of you." I relax a little more and take his hand in mine to lead him over to the bed. *What the heck am I going to do when I get him there? Run maybe.*

He grabs both of my wrists into his giant hand and tosses me to the floor like a rag doll. "I know what you're trying to do, you dirty whore."

I scramble away until my back hits the bed.

He's pulling his belt loose, folding it in his palms. "We are going to have some fun with this." Sweat is dripping down his face.

I wrap my arms around my head. The *crack*! The sting. It's like nothing I have ever felt before. "Help!"

Crack! Sting.

"*Aaaahhh*." Through the blur of tears, I can see he's got his dick in one hand.

Crack! Sting.

"Help me! Mama!" *Crack*! Sting. "H-help . . ."

"Izabel. Wake up."

My eyes spring open. Rachel is standing above me, shaking my shoulders. I blink a few times from my spot on the floor. I roll onto my side and vomit.

Somewhere between my coughing fit and my river of tears, Rachel leans down and embraces my shivering body. "Don't worry, dear. I'll help you through this. Take as much time as you need."

The dam has broken. The last four years, the last ninety years, it all comes pouring out of me. I . . . Eve didn't deserve that. Why didn't Charlie come back to save her? This cycle of abuse ends here—in this room.

"I'd like to try those breathing exercises now." I sniffle into her shoulder.

Rachel presses me closer to her and whispers softly in my ear, "Of course."

10

I give myself a final once-over in the mirror. *Yes, I look good.* I'm looking forward to seeing Natalie tonight. We have barely spoken in the last couple of weeks, let alone seen each other. She's been consumed with getting her event together. But now it's here—a Friday night out not surrounded by politicos. I'm secretly happy—thrilled, actually—that Bo is out of town again. He wouldn't have enjoyed himself anyway. He's never appreciated Natalie's artistic vision.

I wrap an oversized scarf around my neck for the finishing touch to my signature autumn look: skinny jeans, blazer, and a deep V-neck white T-shirt. From my jewelry cabinet, I grab a pair of chandelier earrings.

There it is . . . the little blue box that, even tucked away out of sight, has weighed on me like an avalanche; the box that defines our marriage. *You should have left*, it whispers.

Marriage is about commitment, a voice in my head trills. *It requires hard work and compromise. Aren't you strong enough to hold your vows? He needs you, he needs you, he needs you . . .*

My cell rings, snapping me out of my reverie. It's the car service. The proverbial blue box that harbors so much pain and confusion gets filed in the back of my brain and cabinet once again.

"Hi there, I'll be right down." I snap the cabinet door closed.

☐ ☐ ☐

Natalie has outdone herself. The gallery looks incredible. The floor has been tiled with blood-red carpet squares, and mesh panels adorned with paintings and photographs hang in an airborne maze, suspended from the ceiling by oversized chains. She must be thrilled by the turnout. A bevy of art connoisseurs and casual collectors are spread throughout the gallery, staking their early claims.

She spots me from across the room, frantically waves to catch my attention, then holds one finger up to let me know she'll come over soon. I survey the eclectic crowd. A small group of women have gathered around a blown glass piece that, at first glance, resembles a vagina, but I think is supposed to be an exotic flower. They are concentrating on their programs and discussing the adverse effects of sexual misrepresentation in the media. *Maybe it is a vagina?* That must be one of Nat's new pieces.

There is a tall, bald man standing solo, wearing skin-tight leather pants and what I hope is a faux-fur coat. He's holding a large Japanese fan and delicately fanning his face. A miniature Yorkie peeks out of his purse. The pair of them are gazing at a black-and-white photo of a naked black man wearing a penis cage. I'm beginning to notice a theme here. I'm going to need a drink sooner rather than later.

I make my way farther into the gallery and spot several servers floating around, carrying trays with mini crystal tumblers filled with a brilliant emerald-green liquid. They are all impeccably dressed in kaleidoscopic, minuscule dresses. A beautiful brunette stops to offer me a drink, and now that I can see her close up, my mouth drops open. She isn't wearing a dress. She isn't wearing anything at all. Her body is expertly and strategically painted with metallic golds and silvers, scarlet reds and cobalt blues. I take notice of the other servers. They are all body painted. Some have koi fish and apple blossom branches painted from front to back, others have dragons and flames. This is so not my scene. *I'm a little turned on, though. I'm not gonna lie.*

"Would you like to try the signature drink of the evening? It's called the Green Goddess." Her voice is sultry.

I can't help but scan her perfectly toned body from head to toe, and I feel my cheeks start to flush.

"Um, sure. What's in it?" I desperately try not to look at her perky, painted breasts. "Absinthe and a drop of sour apple." She wears a wolfish grin and gives me a wink.

Aside from Nat, I've never had a woman be so forward with me.

I take a tumbler from the tray and give her a shy grin. As she walks away, I can't help but check out her behind. I giggle and take a sip of the Green Goddess.

Leave it to Natalie to serve absinthe. She's either going to sell every piece in the gallery, or this is going to turn into a scene from Caligula. *Oh, this is dangerously tasty though.*

I wallflower for a few minutes and absorb my surroundings. I need to acclimate to the innuendos unfolding around me. Only Natalie can ooze sex so elegantly and with so much style. I'm so proud of her, of her limitless fearlessness, of her ability to just step across the imaginary lines created by society.

And I'm jealous of her too. She's never had to rebel. Her mother, Caroline, always accepted her. If she came home with blue hair, her mother would say, "Oh, that's a lovely shade, dear." One time she came home with a baby raccoon. Caroline just suggested, "Maybe you should bring the mommy home too, so they don't miss each other."

And at fifteen, when Natalie told her mom she was pregnant, Caroline hugged her, tight as a python, as Nat would later describe it, and said, "Don't worry what anyone thinks. We will raise and love this baby together." Natalie had asked me to come along for support that day. I remember crying as I witnessed Caroline's tender, unwavering approval. I'm not sure if I cried because it was so touching, or because I knew I wouldn't have received the same reaction had the tables been turned.

We didn't get a chance to raise that baby. Natalie was in a car accident a couple of months later and miscarried. I missed two weeks of school just lying in bed with her, hoping to offer solace for her loss. Those two weeks of truancy were the furthest I ever got to stepping a toe out of line.

I locate Natalie again. Now she's enveloped by a gaggle of admirers. We lock eyes, and she gives me an adoring smile as if she is reading my thoughts. She excuses herself and trots over.

"There's my girl!" She grabs my face and greets me with a big, sticky kiss. "So, what do you think?"

"Not quite my cup of tea." I tilt my head toward the hanging vagina. "But honestly, you've done a fabulous job, Nat. And you look beyond gorgeous."

Other than a ballerina or a two-year-old girl, nobody but Nat or Sarah Jessica Parker can pull off wearing a pink tutu out in public. Of course, she has accompanied it with a black leather bustier and a pair of five-inch Alexander McQueen's.

"And how do you like the signature drink?" She taps her fingers together in the most mischievous way.

"Absinthe, really? I'm waiting for the orgy to break out."

"Well, a girl can dream, can't she?"

I give her my best prudish, shocked face and gasp loudly, then we both double over in laughter.

The flashes of cameras go off in every direction, blinding us temporarily. There is a gathering of photographers snapping pictures left and right.

"Smile, Natalie!" one shouts.

"Over here!" another pipes up.

She puts her arm around my waist and starts posing. Kissing my cheek. Sticking out her tongue. Turning to the side and kicking her back leg up. Palm over her mouth like she's been caught in the act. When she's had enough, she shoos them away.

"I have to circulate. I'll come and find you again

soon, though. There's someone here I want you to meet. Go mingle. Explore the endless possibilities this room has to offer." She flutters backward into the eagerly awaiting crowd and calls out, "Trust your instincts!"

I'm reminded of my last visit with Rachel. Those were her final words to me. I haven't thought about that in weeks. I take another sip of the Green Goddess and merge into the throng of people, hoping to blend in. Mr. Yorkie Purse ends up beside me and introduces himself. Turns out, he's an interior decorator for the stars, and boy, do they have their quirks, he tells me. The penis photograph, for example, is going to hang in the bedroom of an actor who "may or may not have starred in one of this year's highest-grossing films."

I give him a wink, insinuating that my lips are sealed, even though I have no idea to whom he is referring. I can't even remember the last time I went to see a movie. Movie date night isn't high on Bo's priority list.

I continue through the maze of panels, making small talk and exchanging nods of approval with passers-by. One of the painted girls stops and offers me another drink. I take another from the tray and replace it with my empty glass. *Body paint!* I shake my head.

I stop to investigate one of the paintings in particular. I can't make out what it is. I pull my glasses out of my purse and hold them on the tip of my nose, leaning in close. From afar it looks like peaks of mountains, but as I get closer, I realize it's two ambiguously positioned women. Very Picasso-esque. I get so close to the painting that my nose is almost touching it. I cock my head to one side as I try to figure out what these two women are doing. I'm lost in interpretation, but I step back and . . . *Ah, that's what they're doing.*

"Jones!" Natalie's shout startles me. "I want you to meet someone."

Embarrassment floods over me because I've just been caught ogling a female sixty-nine.

I put my glasses back in my purse and turn to meet Natalie and her guest. "It's you!" I say under my breath.

Natalie crinkles her eyebrows at me but proceeds with her introductions. "Jones, this is Henry Rudolph." *Henry Rudolph.* The man with the eyes I could just dive into.

He smiles and extends his hand. "Nice to see you again, Ms. Jones."

"It's Izabel. Izabel *Carmichael*." An unexpected regret creeps over me as I correct him. Henry tilts his head to one side and looks at me, puzzled. "Natalie fails to remember that I'm not a Jones anymore." I point to my ring finger.

"All the same, it's nice to meet you properly this time."

"Hold up! What's going on? Do you two know each other?" Natalie looks back and forth between Henry and me.

He chuckles. "No, Natalie, Ms. Jon—Mrs. *Carmichael* and I literally ran into each other at a coffee shop a few weeks back."

What is it about this man? I want to run, hide, get as far away from him as I can, bury myself in the deepest hole I can find. But the other part of me wants to jump into his arms and lean my head on his chest and never let go.

Words fail me. All I can do is stare at how impossibly handsome he is and regret even more that I spilled coffee on him. He looks a little different today. He's wearing Clark Kent glasses.

There is a tightening in my groin. I want to run my fingers through that dark-brown hair and get lost in those mesmerizing green eyes . . . and those lips, what would it feel like if he brushed them across my neck?

Over his left shoulder, I see her. Leggy Blonde is strutting in our direction, and I'm overcome with inexplicable jealousy. Before I can blink, she is standing next to him, her arm wrapped around his . . . *again*!

"I was looking for you." Her whiney drawl pierces my eardrums. She leans in close and kisses the side of Henry's beautiful face.

I roll my eyes, hoping neither of them notices, but she turns to Natalie and kisses her square on the lips. *That's it. No more Green Goddess for me. I'm lost.*

"Jones, this is my *friend* Portia, the one I was telling you about." Natalie gives me a salacious grin.

Leggy Blonde—Portia—releases Henry and amorously wraps her arms around Natalie. I look at Henry and rub my temple with pointed fingers. He laughs and grabs my free hand. The electricity I felt when he touched me that day in the coffee shop comes zinging back, and I tense a little.

"I'm . . . confused," is all I can muster.

Henry's brow furrows a little. "Portia's my sister."

"And Portia's my Portia. Now, we are going to find some hors d'oeuvres, aren't we, love?" Nat smiles at Portia.

"Have fun you two."

Natalie leans in and gives me a hug. She whispers in my ear, "How fucking hot is he? You're welcome."

"Nat, it's been a—a great night, but I have to go. Soon."

"Oh no, you don't, Jones! I spent an entire night at your wedding playing nice with the fascists . . . for you! You're not going anywhere, you hear me? Plus, the real party is just getting started." Then she and Portia vanish into the crowds.

"Your friend is tenacious." Henry raises an eyebrow, giving me an amused look.

"Don't forget dramatic—tall, sexy, confident . . . Well, I've seen as much vag and cock as I can take for one night, how about you?"

He grins at me with a mix of surprise and delight. "Agreed. After you, Mrs. Carmichael." He gestures toward two lone lounge chairs off in the corner.

"You know, I guess you can call me Jones if you want."

"Good. C'mon, Jones. Let's grab a seat."

11

Henry and I sit across from each other in the lounge area. I'm struck speechless—again— by his face. His beautiful, gorgeous face. The truth is I don't know how to form a coherent sentence that won't lead to me spilling everything about Rachel and the past life I visited. Of course, he'd think it's insane. I think it's insane. But what if I never see him again? I can't *not* tell him.

"So, how . . ." we say nervously in unison.

"Ladies first."

"How do you know our illustrious Natalie?" I arch an eyebrow in what I hope is a playful look.

"She contacted my grandfather's estate a few months back regarding a painting she was researching. She was very insistent with them, as I'm sure you can attest to." I give him an understanding roll of my eyes.

"The lawyers passed her information along to me, since I was in possession of the piece, and we've been in contact ever since. It seems like Natalie's not one to let people go."

"And you had no problem giving up the painting?"

I am slightly annoyed by his lack of sentiment for his grandfather's painting. Clearly, if Nat wants it, it must be valuable. And he was so quick to sell it?

"At first, I wasn't interested in her offer because it was a very special piece for him. I asked him once why he held onto it. Why he didn't sell that one like he had so many others. All he said was 'I need to keep it. It will be seen one day when the time is right.' After talking to Natalie, listening to how excited she was, how much research she'd done . . . I don't know, it just seemed right, I guess."

"Oh." Now I feel bad. The heat of a blush creeps up my face. "So—uh—how does Portia fit into the picture?"

"Portia was with me when I first met Natalie. And the rest is history."

There's a comfortable pause in our conversation. We sit in silence and let the music and the voices wash between us for a moment. It's not unpleasant just sitting here with him.

"My turn," he says after a moment. "What's your story, Jones? How do *you* know our illustrious Natalie, as you so perfectly put it?" Now it's his turn to raise an eyebrow at me.

"Oh . . . no, nothing like that! Nat and I are practically sisters. We grew up together in Milwaukee. Then, when I got accepted to UChicago, she jumped at the opportunity to come to the city with me."

"You know, Jones, something profound happened that day in the coffee shop between us. I haven't been able to stop thinking about you. And now . . . here we are." He looks at me with those deep, penetrating green eyes. They're so alluring. It's easy to stare, to feel that look resonate like the thrum of a bow, of a harp string, throughout my body.

I break eye contact and pick at an imaginary pull in the fabric of my chair. Clearing my throat, I suggest, "Why don't you show me your grandfather's painting? I'd love to see it, if you wouldn't mind."

He hops out of his chair, extending his hand for me to hold. "I'd love to show you. Now, I don't want you to be disappointed. It's not as risqué as the others. I know how much you enjoyed the penis photos."

"Oh, shut it." I giggle and give him a playful punch on the shoulder.

I let him lead me by the hand through the maze of art and people. The feeling of his palm in mine makes me giddy, like a high-schooler on a first date. He stops suddenly and walks behind me, playfully placing his hands over my eyes, bringing his mouth to my ear.

"I think we need a big reveal after I talked the painting up so much. Don't you?"

"Yes." My voice is barely a whisper.

We walk a few more steps with his front pressed into my back. I can feel the warm sweetness of his breath.

"You ready?"

Shivers resonate down my spine as he speaks, and his lips brush my ear. All I can do is nod. If I try to speak, I'll moan.

He uncovers my eyes, runs his hands down my arms, and places them on my waist. I blink a few times until the room comes back into focus. The painting is of a beautiful, naked young woman sitting on the edge of a chair. She looks over her shoulder, so you can just see the profile of her face. Her back is long and lean, pale and smooth, with a delicate string of pearls cascading it.

I cup my hand over my mouth and try to muffle the strange little sobs that are coming out of me. Tears begin to roll down my cheeks, and even though I'd love to excuse myself, I am rooted there, fixated.

"What is it?" Concern fills Henry's voice.

I try, but fail, to unclench my throat enough to speak. I have to hide my face, hide the blubbering mess I'm devolving into. Henry embraces me but doesn't say a word. He just lets me cry for a moment.

After a long minute, he lifts my chin so he can see my face. "Hey, if it's that horrible, I'll tell Natalie to take it down."

"I don't know why I'm crying. It's just . . . you're going to think I'm crazy, but I have a story for you."

"Well, I like a little crazy now and then." He smiles down at me.

"I'm going to need another drink for this. And you're going to want one too." We head back to the lounge area, Green Goddesses in hand.

An hour and many drinks later, I finish telling Henry about my regression experience, how Natalie bailed on me but I still went, about the squeaky hallway, and Rachel, and about Eve and Charlie and how absolutely in love they were, how passionate their lovemaking was and how real it felt when I was there. I explained that Charlie would paint her each time he came to see her. He told her she was his magnum opus. I smile at the memory of their bodies moving together as one. I can feel the cold paint of his brush, phantom strokes all over my body.

"And one day he just left. The last words he said to her were, 'I love you forever, Eve,' and she never saw him again. And .. you look so much ... When I bumped into you in the coffee shop, I couldn't believe my eyes. I had just had this incredible out-of-body experience, then there you were. You look so much like Charlie, and I just had this feeling, this ... urge ... I wanted to wrap my arms around you and tell you."

Tears are once again falling freely down my face. He moves closer to me, so our knees are touching, and wipes my moist cheeks with the pad of his thumb.

"You think I'm crazy, right? I think I'm crazy. Don't worry, I know it's nuts." A slow grin grows across his face.

"So, you're the one?"

"What?"

"When I was young, my grandfather and I would talk for hours. About everything— history, geography, art, philosophy, and love. He was an accomplished artist. He'd seen so much of the world. No matter what we were talking about, he always used to say to me, 'One day you will find your Forever Eve,' but I never paid much attention to that. Near the end of his life, he was bedridden, which was very difficult for him. He'd fall in and out of consciousness, and I'd just sit with him for hours, day after day. And sometimes he'd talk. Most of what he said was incoherent. One day, he pulled me close and whispered, 'Tell Eve I am truly sorry. She lived in my heart every day.' I never understood what that meant. Until now.

He left me that painting in his will and, like I told you, when Natalie called about acquiring it, I just knew it was time. To let it go. Let it be seen. I don't think you're crazy. I think we were meant to meet."

I don't know if it's the booze, or this incredible love story, or sheer lust, but I leap forward, knocking Henry back in his seat, and I kiss him, really kiss him. At first, he doesn't reciprocate, then he relaxes and lets my tongue discover his delicious mouth. He clenches the nape of my neck and deepens our kiss. I crawl into his chair and straddle him, wrapping my fingers through his hair, tugging gently. He groans deep in his throat and pulls my head back. He moves his lips down to the base of my neck and kisses every inch of my skin back up to my ear.

I pull away, breathless, and put my hand over my lips in protest. I look around the room to see if anyone noticed, but the atmosphere has changed. The lights are dim and red, and the music is an ethereal, repetitive electronica beat. The mood is no longer of collection and appraisal. It's carnal.

I look down at Henry, his breathing still heavy. "I am so sorry. That was inappropriate of me. It just felt—"

"I know. I felt it too."

Our eyes stay connected for a few seconds longer.

"Let's . . . let's go find the girls. Come on." He stands, effortlessly lifting me with him, and holds me tight until my feet are back on the floor. We pause awkwardly, adjusting any articles of clothing that shifted during our illicit moment of weakness before we walk into the crowd.

We manage to track down Natalie and Portia at the back of the building where the panels have been moved to make room for a dance floor. The body-painted women are no longer serving drinks. They're moving fluidly around in sensual dance, light reflecting off their metallic paint.

"Jooonnneess!" Natalie rushes over and throws her arms around my neck. "I saw you," she teases. Before the weight of her words can pull me under, she plunges on. "Looked like you were having fun! You finally let *loose*!" She grabs my hand, twirls herself around like a ballerina, then grabs Henry's. "Come on, you two. Dance floor, now!"

We are pulled toward the shivering, swaying pool of dancers, and threatened to be carried away on the waves of their rhythms when Natalie drops our hands and ceases to be our anchor.

She disappears into the swirling crowd, and her crowing fades into the tempo. Colors and noises and lights press in on me. Henry wraps his arms around my torso, and we fall into the pulsing beat. We move like that for hours, never letting go of each other.

12

Oh, man. I feel horrible. *Why did I drink so much last night?* I think I need to throw up. I lie still for a moment, debating if I need to rush to the toilet or not.

Shit! What time is it? Shit! Brunch with Tippy. I jump out of bed and look at the clock.

10 a.m. *Ugggh*, I have to meet her in an hour.

The room starts spinning. *Is it a hundred degrees in here? I'm definitely going to puke.* I run to the bathroom and make it just in time. It's like I'm being exorcized. *Damn you, Green Goddess.* I start to pray to the alcohol gods. *Please let me feel better soon. I promise I will never drink again.*

I cradle my head in my hands and lean against the cold porcelain with my elbows.

What time did I get home last night? *How* did I get home last night? Only flashes of the night come back to me—dancing, sweating, kicking off my shoes . . . *Shit*! I kissed Henry. Visions of him splash through my mind—those sweet, full lips, his fingers gently tugging at my hair, his arousal against my thigh.

What have I done?

□ □ □

I trudge into Chez Nous at 11:10 a.m. The maître d'
greets me kindly. "Good morning, Mrs. Carmichael. Let
me show you to your table." He leads me to a sunlit
table tucked near the back with a view of their garden.
Only the best for the Carmichaels.

Tippy, ever happy in her role as next-tier clientele
in another one of her Chanel suits, looks her usual immaculate self. "There you are. I thought you had forgotten about me." She stands and gives me her double
cheek air-kiss. "Izabel, darling, you look like hell." She
assesses me suspiciously.

"I-I-I seem to have caught a bug." I clear my throat
and sniffle for effect.

"Yes, well, I have the perfect remedy for that. Sit."

She reaches into her purse and pulls out a pill bottle, shakes a few out, and hands them to me. "Take
these."

She pours me a Bloody Mary from her pitcher, and I
don't question it. I toss the multi- colored pills to the
back of my throat and wash them down with the ice-
cold vodka and tomato juice.

"Okay, let's get down to business." She slides a piece
of paper across the table. "Here's the agenda of events
for the next few weeks that you'll need to attend with
me." I quickly glance over it:

Saint Frances Hospital pediatric wing ribbon cutting

*National Association of Women's Business Develop-
ment Center grand opening Chicago's Youth Shelter gala*

I skip down to the end and see:

Abused Women's Coalition fundraiser

My head is pounding. I blink, trying to make sure I look like I'm studiously examining the entire schedule. Grand opening, ribbon cutting, gala, photo op . . .

Abused Women's Coalition fundraiser Abused Women's Coalition fundraiser

"Is everything okay, Izabel?"

I un-hunch myself from the list and try to unscrew my face. "Just feeling a little ill, that's all."

"Have another drink, dear. You'll feel better in no time." She swirls the ice around her glass. Tippy spends the next forty-five minutes explaining the event process to me as we eat our Cobb salads. The men usually don't attend. It's important that the wives have individual exposure but not overshadow the topics being covered on the campaign.

"Always smile and deflect any negative questions by answering, *America is too great to dream small dreams.*"

I'm trying to listen. I really am.

"Excuse me, Mrs. Carmichael." The maître d' interrupts her monologue of good governor's wife behavior. "There's a call for you."

Tippy doesn't believe in carrying a cell phone. If it's so important to speak with her, whoever needs her will find her. She excuses herself and follows the maître d' to the front.

I grab the newspaper from the next table. Maybe Natalie's event made it into the arts section. I flip through the sections, hoping—dreading—a glimpse of last night. News, sports, business . . . Wait! That was Bo. I turn back a couple of pages, and up in the right-hand corner is a photo of Jack Carmichael and another man shaking hands, and set in the background is Bo. He has his arms wrapped around a tall, slim brunette. My heart sinks to the pit of my stomach. I'm going to throw up again. Everything around me disappears. I'm frozen, staring at the photo for who knows how long. I don't notice Tippy standing above me.

She chuckles, a well-practiced sound that, genuine or not, always sounds canned. "Oh, darling, thick skin is a prerequisite when you marry a Carmichael." She moves around to her seat, places her napkin back on her lap, and stabs another bite of salad. "That's not the last photo you'll see. You'll find ways to keep your imagination at bay. That's the ticket. A good personal trainer or masseuse always proves to be a wonderful distraction."

What is she saying? What is she *saying*? Is she suggesting . . . That's her son! What does she mean by *distraction*?

"Darling, don't look at me like I'm some damsel in distress. I have total control over my life. I make the decisions necessary to maintain the splendors I require to keep me happy."

I gape at her, wide-eyed. "I'm sure it's nothing." I manage to say the words as though my heart is not torn into a thousand pieces.

"Of course, dear." She gives me a non-committal smile. "Now, where were we?"

Tippy and I say goodbye. She offers to have her driver take me home, but I decline. I need to walk for a bit. I need some fresh air to clear my head. Somewhere between Elm Street and Burnaby Avenue, I decide I'll feel better if I hear Bo's voice. But the call goes straight to voice mail.

"Hi, honey. It's me ... Izabel. Just checking in to see how your trip is going. Call me when you get the message. I love you. See you tomorrow."

It's nothing. You'll see. You don't even have a right to be mad.

Just as I put my phone in my pocket, it rings. I grab for it and answer. "Bo?"

"Henry."

"Henry?"

"I'm crushed! You've forgotten me already?"

"No, no, that's not it at all. I'm just expecting a call from my husband. How—how did you get my number?"

"Natalie gave it to me. I hope you don't mind?"

That woman is going to send me to my grave one day.

"No, not at all. How are you?"

He laughs. "Better than when I first woke up. How are you, Jones? Feeling rough?"

"Yeah, it's been a rough morning for me. Last night was pretty crazy."

"Yes, your friend sure knows how to show a New Yorker a good time."

"You have no idea. Listen, Henry, last night ... that was some very uncharacteristic behavior from me. I hope I didn't ... um, offend you."

He laughs. "Quite the opposite. I was wondering if you'd join me for dinner tonight."

Tingles run through my body as visions of our kiss resurface. I shake my head. No, I can't see him again.

Whatever Tippy meant about distractions and decisions, no. Just no. That's not me, and that's not my marriage.

"Henry, I had a good time last night too—an unbelievable night, actually. But I'm married. I don't think meeting again would be a good idea."

He's silent for a minute. "You're probably right. I don't want to cause you any problems."

For a moment, I just keep walking, the phone pressed up to my ear, dead air between us.

Electric, aching silence.

"It's just that—"

"Henry, I . . . I can't. Please understand."

"I do, Jones. I apologize for even suggesting it. I'll be in town for another week or so finishing up some business. If you need anything, don't hesitate to call me, please."

"Thank you. And Henry, it was a pleasure to meet you."

"Izabel Jones, the pleasures were all mine."

We hang on the phone in silence for a few seconds more, then the line goes dead, and I deflate like a balloon. Every step feels difficult. I'm so far from home.

I told him my story. I've solved the mystery, and now it's over. It has to be over. I need to move on and concentrate on getting Bo and I back on track.

My phone rings again, making me jump. "Bo?"

"No, it's me, you dirty slut." Natalie's sing-song tone is more than I can handle, and I swallow hard as she continues. "I didn't think you had it in you."

"I don't have anything in me, Natalie. Last night should have never happened, and it will never happen again." I try to play down the pain in my voice.

"So, I guess that's a no to a double date tonight?"

"Uh, yeah, that would be a big no." I don't have the patience for her right now.

"Okay, suit yourself." She coughs the word "boring" into the phone. "You have to admit last night was RI-DIC-U-lousss. Don't try and hide it. I know you had fun too."

"I will admit that level of fun is way out of my league."

"Yes, I forgot Boring Bo doesn't like to party. Where is Mr. Wonderful this weekend, anyway?"

"Natalie, please, can you just be nice for once? He's my fucking husband."

"Fine, fine! But if you change your mind, and you want to get out for a drink, we're going to be at 2Kats."

"Thanks for the offer, but Bo will be home from Maine tomorrow afternoon, and I don't want to feel anything like I did today."

"Have it your way, Jones. You know it feels good. I'll call you tomorrow. Love you."

"Love you too, Nat. Bye."

I look at the clock on my phone—almost two p.m. What am I going to do for the rest of the day? I should go into the office and catch up on some patient files. It's Saturday. No one else will be there.

I will walk there. It's only twenty blocks. The cool, crisp air is doing wonders for my headache, even if my legs feel leaden. I normally would relish this time to myself. I'm never alone. If it's not galas and photo ops with Bo, it's ladies' luncheons and charity events with Tippy. So, why is this time I usually crave making me feel so alone?

I walk head down, block after block, counting the cracks in the sidewalk. The wind is picking up, so I pause at a shop window to adjust my cardigan and scarf. Tippy was right, I do look like hell. Maybe a facial should be on the agenda for today as well.

I notice a beautiful potted orchid in the shop window. The white and fuchsia flowers cascade down the support rod, and I'm immediately reminded of my first few dates with Bo. He would bring me a single orchid on every date, each one a different color, with a little note attached that he would recite to me, explaining what each one symbolized.

I can hear his words like he said them yesterday. "Yellow for friendship and new beginnings. A blue orchid is rare, symbolizing rarity like your ability to let anything roll off your back. A pink orchid for joy and happiness—just like I feel whenever I'm with you or even think of you. A white orchid—innocence, beauty, and elegance."

The day I knew I fell in love with him, he brought a bouquet of all the colors tied together with a shiny purple sash, and the note read:

Orchids are considered symbols of love because they can grow under the most grueling conditions but bloom the most exquisite and vibrant flowers, showering the earth with the hope that all can be overcome. The rarer the orchid, the deeper the love. You are my rare, exquisite, and vibrant flower, Izabel, and you've brought me hope. I love you.

I inhale the cold breeze with a new sense of purpose. My Bo is still in there, he just needs help finding his way. Enough with his father. Enough with my petty complaints about his travel schedule. Enough of his jaded mother. Enough of past lives and looking elsewhere to fill a hole only a husband can fill. I'll surprise him tomorrow when he gets home—rose petals, candles, strawberries, and champagne. And I'll stop by La Perla and buy some new sexy lingerie. No one can save my marriage but me.

13

I wake feeling energized. My blinds are open, and glorious sunlight streams through the window. Today is the dawning of a new day for Bo and me. I spring out of bed, pull my hair up, and head straight for the shower. The warm water trickles down my body. I haven't felt this good in days. I shave all my girly bits and loofah my skin with the sea sponge and jasmine-vanilla body wash I bought yesterday. Smooth and soft, I hop out of the shower and wrap up in my plush robe, ready to finish my last few tasks.

Hair done ... *check.*

Smokin' hot lingerie ... *check.*

Champagne and strawberries chilling ... *check.*

Now I just need to sprinkle my rose petals down the hall toward the bedroom, and I'm all done. I should send Natalie a message to tell her I'm busy this afternoon, but when I rummage through my purse to get my phone, it's dead. *Crap!*

I plug my phone into the charger by the microwave, and after a couple of seconds, it grabs a charge and my message notification pings. I hope I didn't miss any calls from Bo.

I have two new messages, the electronic voice tells me. "First message sent at 12:10 a.m. from Natalie."

"Wooo . . . Jones! You are missing a fucking awesome night. The place is packed. Henry is asking about you. He's got it bad, girl. Come overrr. Okay, bye . . . love you."

I giggle. Natalie is indeed a force to be reckoned with. I smile at the thought of Henry, then shake it off. I can't let either of them sidetrack me right now.

"Next message sent at 1:50 a.m.," says voice mail lady. "From . . ." Dammit, I missed a call from Bo. I can hear a woman laughing and a man's voice, but I can't really make out what they're saying. He must have pocket dialed me. In the middle of the night?

I replay it and listen closely this time. A woman's giggle. Then I hear Bo's voice, "God, you're . . . been . . . to fuck you all night."

I drop the phone and cover my ears, hoping I didn't just hear what I think I heard. It has to be wrong. Has to be. I scramble to pick up the phone. *Message deleted.* Wait! What? *Shit, shit, shit!*

Snatching the bottle of champagne out of the fridge, I pop the cork and take a long swig. I go back to my room and throw on my robe then drag myself back to the dining room and plop down at the table.

Stop thinking about it, Izabel. I'm sure he has a reasonable explanation. Does he?

Bastard!

I drain the last bit of liquid out of the bottle.

"Izabel, I'm home!"

"I'm in the dining room." My reply is sweetened by the bubbly.

I hear him drop his bags and round the corner to the dining room. When he sees me, his smiling face turns to concern.

"Have you been crying?"

"Well, aren't you Mr. Observant?"

He scowls. Not the answer he was looking for. "What's wrong?"

"Oh, I don't know, maybe I stubbed my toe. Or maybe I didn't hear from my husband for two days. Or, here's a good one, maybe you had sex with another woman last night."

His earlier look of concern has now become indignant. "Excuse me?"

"Bo, please! Don't play me for an idiot. I heard the voice mail."

"What voice mail?"

"You pocket dialed me in the middle of the night, and I heard you with her."

"I don't appreciate your accusation, Izabel."

"I don't care if you appreciate it. I heard you!"

"At least let me hear the voice mail so I have an understanding of what it is I'm defending myself against."

"Oh, you're good. You can't hear it because I deleted it . . . by mistake!" I shout. His glare oozes anger from my outburst. "Was it her?"

"Was it who, Izabel?"

"The woman from the newspaper." My voice cracks.

He looks at me and his eyes narrow, deepening the lines on his forehead. "Seriously, what are you talking about now? Do you hear yourself?"

"I saw you in yesterday's paper with your arms around a brunette."

He eyes me contemptuously, his fingers flexing. "Izabel, you are starting to piss me off. You spend all day psychoanalyzing nut jobs and now you're starting to sound like one."

I huff and stand up out of my chair, ready to face down the bear. "I don't psychoanalyze nut jobs all day. I help people and assess habitual behaviors. Why am I even— Stop diverting from the real issue! Let's talk about 'I've been waiting to fuck you all night!'"

Then it hits me. *Think about it, Izabel. All the weekend business trips, not answering his phone.* His words from a few weeks ago scream in my ear: *You're not some slut I fuck.* I'm so stupid.

"Your mother might be okay with your father disappearing every weekend for that, but not me. Maybe people slip up, and if it was just this once, then fine ... well, not fine, but we could get past this. But I will not tolerate this for our entire marriage."

"Baby, come on." His smirk only acts to irritate the rage boiling inside me. "It's nothing. You are completely overreacting."

"I'm overreacting? Overreacting? Are you kidding me?" *Don't do something you'll regret. Don't do it. Don't do it.* "Well then, you should be perfectly fine when I tell you I kissed someone."

The condescending smile dismantles itself and something sinister builds behind his eyes.

What have you done? Stand your ground. Do it, or you're dead.

He's silent for a few minutes, his breathing steadied. Then he walks toward me, closing my strategically calculated distance. He looks down at me, gives me a half-amused grin, and shakes his head. My heart is pounding out of my chest. I can't tell if he's angry or relieved.

Before I can react, he turns to walk away. A huge sigh leaks out of me.

He's just going to leave? We're not going to discuss this anymore? Then with the force of a hammer, his right hand swings up and he backhands me across the face, catapulting me into the wall. The back of my skull stings and my joints jolt as I hit the floor. I scurry into the corner and slide into a ball, knees tucked to chest, one hand thrust out as he rushes toward me.

"Bo! Stop, please!"

He grabs me under the armpits and drags me up, lifts me against the wall so my feet are suspended from the ground. I am too scared to even cry. I just stare into his eyes in hopes that magically or telepathically he'll listen to me.

"You think you can fuck around on me?" His voice is hoarse. He lowers me back to my feet and rests one hand on the wall above my shoulder. Looking down at my breasts, he presses his hips into me. "It would be a shame to let this little outfit go to waste, now wouldn't it?" He trails his index finger from my collarbone down to my cleavage. I tighten the sash of my robe, but he grabs my wrists in one of his hands and thrusts them above my head.

"Bo, please, you're hurting me." I sob.

Pinching my chin between his fingers, he pushes my head to one side, exposing my neck. A moan escapes his mouth, then he plants his lips on my neck and begins to lick and bite at my skin. "You smell so good, Izabel. Come with me."

He tightens his grip around my wrists and drags me into the bedroom. He strips me of my robe, then pushes me face first onto the bed. In one swift move, he undoes his belt and pulls it through the loops of his pants.

I whirl and flail, instinctively raising my hands to cover my face. "Bo! Don't hit me!"

"Shhh. I'm not going to hit you, baby."

He straddles me and grabs my wrists again, tying the belt around them. He hoists my arms above my head and fastens the belt to the headboard. Gazing down at me, he brushes the hair away from my face.

"If you fight me, Izabel, it will only be worse for both of us." Tears flow down my face. I can no longer contain them.

"Please . . ." I whisper, hoping he will snap out of his rage and realize what he is about to do to me . . . to his wife.

☐ ☐ ☐

The scent that used to make me swoon and smile is now wretched and making me vomit. I need this stench of him off of me. Mist from the running shower envelopes the bathroom. My lungs feel heavy as they fill with wet heat. The reflection in the mirror is disappearing, and I'm not entirely sure it's because of the steam. Is that even me? Who have I become?

I grab my head between my hands "Get off! Get off me!" I screamed. Why didn't he listen to me?

My eyelid is starting to close over now from the force of the blow. I trace my fingers down the puffy black-and-blue abrasion that has surfaced on my upper cheekbone. My gaze scans over my naked body and I discover a multitude of bruises on my thighs and bite marks on my neck. *Ouch*, my head is throbbing.

I rub my wrists, and his words shriek through my ears. "I'm the only one who gets to fuck you. Do you understand?" His whispered assurance, "See, that wasn't that bad, baby," plays over and over in my mind, making my entire body jolt, and I almost heave again.

I'm pruned and shaking, and the simple task of wrapping a towel around myself proves to be a challenge. I swallow the big lump that has formed at the back of my throat and run to grab clothes randomly from my drawers. I throw them in one crumpled ball into a gym bag and quickly pull on the sweats and a hoodie I tossed to the side. I tug on my UGGs and haul my gym bag and purse over my shoulder. Up on my tiptoes, I quietly make my way down the hall.

I peek my head into the dining room. He's at the table. In front of him are a crystal tumbler and a bottle of tequila. He looks up, regarding me with submissive apathy, his face pale, eyes red and swollen.

"Are you leaving?" His voice is barely audible. I can't bring myself to answer, so I nod.

"Don't go." His voice cracks, and tears well up in his eyes.

It's killing me to see him like this. It's crazy, but I want to go to him. *Tell him it's going to be okay. He needs you. Look at him.*

Leave. NOW.

"Goodbye, Bo." I turn to walk away, but my legs are heavy. "Izabel, please . . ."

I freeze as the irony of his words hits me. I'm a foot from the door, and I hear him get up and stride toward me. I look back. He's walking slowly toward me, arms out, wide-eyed and tearful. I slash my arm out in front of me and he stops and drops his arms to his sides. He surrenders, and I walk out the door.

14

I stand on the concrete stoop, leaning on the inside of the screen, waiting for the door to open. *Shit!* I clumsily grab for the oversized sunglasses in my purse. I never thought these ugly things Nat gave me would come in handy.

"Who is it?" I hear Mom's sweet voice, and the door swings open. She doesn't say a word, just pulls me in and hugs me tight as I start to bawl.

"Oh, Mommy."

"It's okay, honey. You're home now." Her supportive tone makes me cry harder, and I know I don't have to explain anything to her yet. "There, there, sweetie." Mom hushes me as she gently rubs my back.

I detach myself from her and take a step back. I push my glasses back into my hair and nod my head, confirming her questioning look. She gasps then quickly composes herself. I know she wants to be strong for me.

"Come with me." She holds out her hand, leads me to the spare bedroom, and places my bag and purse on the floor. "Lie down, my sweet girl. I'll make you some tea."

I slouch down on the bed, pull one boot off, and toss it across the room. My foot hits the floor like it's filled with cement. I try to lift my other leg, but I don't have the energy. Exhaustion prevails and I lie back and pull the flower-covered comforter over me. I'm released of the adrenaline that has consumed by body over the last few hours. Turning onto my side, I assume my familiar cocoon position. I'm already half-asleep when Mom comes back. She places the mug on the bedside table and kisses my forehead.

"Sleep well, sweet girl. I love you."

The house is dark when I wake. I find Mom in her recliner, reading. Her face shines from the corner lamp's glow. It's almost too much right now just to plod to the couch and curl into the corner. Mom lowers her recliner, leans forward, and strokes my hair.

"I've made you some chicken soup, darling. You'll feel better once you eat."

I know my mother is not suggesting that eating chicken soup will erase the horror I married in to, but it's her way of saying she will wait as long as she needs to for me to tell her what's happened. I'll spare her the gory details. There are just some things a mother doesn't need to know.

I start to cry again. Will this flood of tears ever dry up?

"Oh, Mom. I'm so confused. How can someone be so cruel to the person they love? He was my world."

"Darling, I am so sorry. I should have been more supportive. I honestly had no idea it was this bad." She gets up from her chair to snuggle in beside me. "How long has this been happening?" She sounds stern and protective, as a mother should when her daughter shows up at her doorstep with a black eye.

I hide my face and shake my head, unwilling to answer. I am too ashamed to admit it.

Slowly, as she rubs my back in that soothing way only mothers can, I feel myself relaxing. *Everything will be okay eventually,* she tells me with every long, tender stroke. I take a focused, purifying breath.

"After Christmas, everything started to become very tense between us."

"But you two were lovely at the Carmichaels' Christmas party," my mother interjects.

"I know, and our New Year's in Maine was magical. It started a couple of weeks later when his dad tried to convince us to postpone the wedding again."

Honestly, if I hadn't put my foot down, I don't think we would have gotten married at all.

The irony is cackling at me—hindsight's little witch.

"That man infuriates me! He did *everything* in his power to make sure Bo was traveling all the time. He was never around to help me with *any* of the planning. It was late one Sunday after he'd been away on a business trip and I was in a bad mood. I shouldn't have raised my voice, but I was so frustrated and . . . I just missed him. He was tired and didn't want to argue about the wedding again, and when he tried to leave the room, I grabbed his arm, but when he wiggled out of my grip . . . it was an accident. He didn't mean to hit me. He even cried afterward."

Mom doesn't say a word and continues to rub my back as I tell my story. I glimpse her out of the corner of my eye to gauge her reaction. She's pensive, which surprises me. I'm not sure what I expected her reaction to be. I think I wanted her to be furious. If she hated him, this situation would be much easier for me. It would be validation for me to hate him as well.

"Go on, honey. I'm here to listen, not judge." Her tender smile urges me to continue. "As the weeks and months went on leading up to the wedding, the business trips became more frequent. And so did the . . . accidents."

As I talk, it's like I'm painting a picture of myself—of someone I used to be. A woman who refused to believe there was anything wrong with her husband. *Her* Bo wasn't abusive. He was kind and gentle and loving. *Her* Bo was buckling under the enormous pressure of a political family and a tyrant father. She—I, once upon a time—didn't help the situation. The picture of that deluded, terrified, confused girl swims in my vision and morphs into him—the wrath in his eyes just a few hours ago, how he so easily degraded me, destroying my trust.

"Oh, Mom, these last few months have been so difficult. If I wasn't walking on eggshells around him, I was making excuses for him. I couldn't talk to anyone. That would have been terrible. To just give up. To act like a victim. It's perplexing! Every time I thought we had found a breakthrough . . . I don't know, it just doesn't make sense."

"You never even spoke to Natalie about this?"

I look over at her in horror. "If Nat knew, she'd kill him."

"Izabel, you can't deal with this on your own. I think you need her, sweetie. She's your best friend. She needs to know what is going on."

Mom's kind-hearted commendation for Natalie triggers me to sob like a baby. I wrap my arms around her and hug her tight like my childhood teddy bear during a thunderstorm.

"You cry all you want, honey. You're entitled to this. Just know this hasn't broken you. In time, you'll realize how much strength you've gained. I think it's time I tell you something I should have years ago."

Curiosity halts my tears. I stare at Mom through glistening eyelashes, trying to focus on her face. For the next hour, I listen intently. My father didn't leave us. In fact, Mom ran away with me. He was so abusive she'd ended up in the hospital a few times—broken nose one time, bruised and broken ribs another. She said she had no choice but to run. Our lives depended on it.

"So you see, darling, I know exactly how you feel, and if I'd thought for one minute that you were going through the same thing . . . well, you wouldn't have to be sitting here with me now." Mom sighs heavily and a few tiny, crystal tears escape her eyes.

I am in a total state of confusion, frayed like an old rope. Angry, proud, lost, oddly skeptical. "Why don't I remember any of this?"

"Oh, honey. I made sure you were never around to witness any of it. You were only four when we left. He was drunk and belligerent one night after I put you to bed. I knew I just had to hold off and endure his wrath until he passed out."

"How did he not find us?"

"Things were much different back then. There was no way of tracking us. No cell phones, no GPS, and he wasn't aware of most of my family members. I got you in the car and started heading east."

"Why Milwaukee?"

"It seemed like the most unassuming place at the time. When we first arrived, I found a women's shelter. They were very helpful. They gave me the resources I needed to stay safe."

"And he never came looking for us?"

"No. He knew he'd better leave us alone." Her smile is filled with mischievous pride.

"Should I even ask?" If I wasn't so freaked out, I might be amused by her secrecy.

"Let's just say I left him a little warning, threatening any future plans to procreate."

"Mother!" She shrugs and smiles. "I think I need to go back to bed."

"Are you upset with me, darling?"

"No. No, of course not. I'm just overwhelmed with everything. My brain can't handle this much information. I need to decompress."

Mom pulls me in for her own comforting hug. The burden that plagued her for the last twenty-three years comes flooding out.

"I'm sorry I wasn't honest with you. I didn't want to taint your outlook on men and relationships. I blame myself for what's happened to you. If I had told you about your father, maybe . . ." Her body folds in a full-blown sob.

"No, Mom, don't. Bo's issues have nothing to do with what you did or did not tell me. I'm glad it was just you and I. Besides, look at what a wonderful job you did on your own. I'm the perfect child." Our tears turn into cathartic laughter. We laugh until our bellies hurt, the cure- all for sorrow.

□ □ □

The next morning, I decide to eat a little breakfast Mom prepared for me. We sit at the kitchen table enjoying our silence. She's reading the paper and I'm ... well, I'm doing nothing. My brain wants to focus on the daisies on her plastic tablecloth and nothing else.

"What would you like to do today, darling?" she asks.

"Actually, I was thinking about doing absolutely nothing today, after I call work. I'm sure Dr. Kennedy is worried." I haven't missed a day since I started my placement with him.

I met Dr. Kennedy at a medical symposium after I completed my undergrad. He was so encouraging and helpful. After only twenty minutes of speaking with me, he offered me a placement at his practice for the duration of my master's. At the time, I remember imagining that's what my father would be like.

Mom peeks up over her glasses and takes a sip of her tea. "I already called him for you. I told him you were ill, and you would most likely be off for a few days, but that I would call him with an update."

She takes another sip of her tea and continues to read her paper as though that was totally normal. I should be annoyed with her for calling my boss like I'm some sick schoolgirl, but it would require me to evoke emotion and I just don't have it in me. Besides, I know it comes from a place of love. She doesn't want me to have to lie to Dr. Kennedy, and I sure as hell am not ready to discuss the truth.

Mom was adamant she was going to take the day off and stay home with me, and as much as I would've loved the comfort of her company, I didn't want her to lose any time off work. Somehow, she still managed to cook a casserole and wash, dry, and fold whatever clothes I had stuffed in my gym bag before she left for her shift.

I take a look at the clock on the stove. Well, I suppose I should get this over with. Maybe I'll get lucky and Nat won't answer. It is only nine a.m.

The favorites list in my contacts only has a few people in it. I guess it will be minus one person now. I stare at Bo's name and fat salty tears catch in my eyelashes. How can I go from speaking to someone every day for the last four years to saying nothing at all? It feels like my right arm has been sawed off. I don't know how to adapt. I don't want to. I want everything to go back to the way it was when we were happy.

You can never go back, a little voice says to me. *If you give in to this, then you tell him what he did was acceptable. Forgivable.*

Dubiously, I run my finger down the screen until I reach Natalie's name. I wipe the tears from my eyes and sniffle a few times to try and ready myself for the inevitable conniption that's about to unfold. The ringing on the other end begins. I cross my fingers, wishing for voice mail.

"Where have you been? I've been calling you since yesterday. I was literally about to get in my car and drive over to your place."

I fight the urge to blubber and spill my guts to her. This is not a conversation I can have over the phone. I'll give her as little information as possible right now, just enough to keep her put until tomorrow. If Nat knew what happened yesterday, let alone over the last few months, she would hunt him down, and the outcome of that wouldn't be good for anyone.

"Nat, I need you to listen to me, okay?" My tone is delicate. "I'm at Mom's. I drove here yesterday."

"Why? What's wrong? What's happened?" The panic in her voice is upsetting.

I can't break down on the phone. "I'll come to your place tomorrow and explain everything to you. Please, I can't go into it right now." I swallow back a sob.

"Jones, you're scaring me. Why are you at your mom's? Tell me what's happened. You can't leave me hanging like this."

I stay silent as I choose my words carefully. "Jones!" she screeches.

"Bo and I had a fight yesterday, and I had no choice but to leave. That's all I can say. I'll be at your place by early evening tomorrow."

"What did that fucker—"

"Natalie, if you love me, you'll be strong for me right now. I'm going to stay at your place for a few days until I sort things out. This isn't about you, Nat. Tomorrow, I promise, you'll know everything. I *need* your patience right now, okay?"

She releases a long, agitated sigh. I know she wants to argue, that it's taking all of her willpower to keep quiet. After a few seconds, she responds, "Fine, but if you aren't at my place by six tomorrow night, I will hunt that asshole down."

"I'll be there. Don't worry. I have to go."

"I love you, Jones."

"I know." I can't stop the tears or the sharp intake of breath as I fight for more words. "I'll see you t-t-to-morrow." I press *end*.

I drop my head onto the kitchen table and cover it up with my hood to block out the light.

Darkness is where I want to be right now. I close my eyes. I've been awake for less than two hours, yet I feel like I haven't slept in days.

I drift in and out of a nostalgic haze—visions of Bo, his tender smile and loving eyes.

We're hand in hand on a boardwalk. The wind is cool, but the sun is shining. We've just exchanged a couple of quips. He takes me in his arms and twirls me around. I look up into the sky. The clouds are moving fast and turning gray. Darkness is looming and torren-tial rains start to fall. When I look back into Bo's eyes, they've turned black. His grip around me is strangling. I gasp, trying to get air. He's like a python—the more I struggle, the tighter he squeezes. I try to protest, but my breath is stunted. "*No!*" I finally manage to scream and flail.

"Izabel. Izabel. Wake up. You're having a night-mare."

I open my eyes to find my mother standing over me, overcome with worry. The kitchen is no longer filled with light. It's dusk. I must have slept here all day. I jump from my seat and wrap my arms around her.

"Oh, Mom, I think . . . I think my heart is broken. How could he do this to me?" I weep on her shoulder.

Eventually, she carefully peels away from my clutch,

and I can see her face, creased with worry and love and sadness, and the hard, weary lines of determination.

"Call him, darling. You need to know why. Otherwise this will consume you, and you're too beautiful a person to live with hatred and regret. You may not like what he has to say to you, and you might not even believe him, but you need resolution." She looks at my cell phone on the kitchen table and gestures for me to pick it up. "Go to your bedroom. Have some privacy."

I'm not ready at all to hear his voice, but Mom is right. I need to know. Not next week, not next year. Now. I sit on my bed and stare at his name on the screen, then hesitantly press the *call* button.

"Izabel." I hear his voice on the other end before the first ringtone finishes.

My body immediately tenses. I'm stricken with fear-pain-anger. I don't know if I can go through with this. The enormity of what he has done to me comes flooding back.

"Izabel. Please say something. Come home to me."

The desperation behind his every sob is paralyzing. I still can't find the courage to respond. I listen to his faltered breathing on the other end.

"Why?" It's the only syllable I can choke out.

"Please, come home so we can talk, so you can see how much I love you. I never meant to hurt you."

Above all, even after everything he's done to me, what riddles my mind is the other woman. He needs to admit it. I can't stand the lie he left hanging.

"Admit to the affair, and I will come home tomorrow and *talk* to you." Even the bargaining chip doesn't stop the tears brimming in my eyes.

After an excruciatingly long pause, he clears his throat. "Yes," he says.

Tears drip down my face. "Yes *what*?" I will not make this easy for him.

"Izabel, don't make me say it."

I'm overcome with liberation. The pain behind his cries gives me strength to stand my ground, to challenge him. "Yes what?"

When he finally responds, his words are barely a whisper. "Yes, I had an affair, but—"

"Fine." I cut him off curtly. "I'll be at the house by four." I press *end* before he has a chance to interject, and then I throw my phone against the wall.

I toss and turn all night, wishing for the sun not to rise. My room is too bright even through the blinds. Sunrise breaks over my battle day. I will be wounded whatever the outcome and retreat under the blanket to my self-imposed quarantine searching for . . . what?

Clarity . . . escape . . . relief from my ensuing reality.

The door creaks open, and Mom pokes her head into my room. "Can I make you some breakfast, honey?"

I groan from under my covers.

She sits at the edge of my bed and slowly reveals my head. "What time are you leaving today?"

I don't want to answer, because then it will be true that I have to face him. I pull the covers over my face again. I hear her sigh as she uncovers me.

She rubs my flushed, bruised cheek with the back of her hand. "You know you can come right back home if you need to." She gets up to leave then pauses. "I want you to listen to me. You need to be strong and confident, just as I know you are. He knows he screwed up and that he's losing the best thing that's ever happened in his life. Now you need to show up and prove it to him."

"Okay. I'll be out in a few minutes." I give her a labored smile.

I pull on yesterday's clothes from the pile at the bottom of my bed and meet her at the·front door. We don't exchange a single word, but the tender kiss she plants on my forehead is the reassurance I need.

I wave goodbye to Mom as she drives away in her battered old car to her little job in her small, quaint town. Everything she's done, everything she's accomplished, seems so much brighter in this new context. The house feels a little larger, the yard a little more stately. This is the life of a person who crawled and clawed her way off the floor, bruised and broken— literally—and made a run for it. A run for a better life. This life.

15

I stand with my back against the wall by the entrance of the dining room. I need strategically placed distance between us for my peace of mind. Although, I know in my heart, he won't hurt me again. Bo sits at the table with his head slumped into his hands.

"When—when did it start?" I ask.

It doesn't matter that I should have known, probably did know. It doesn't matter that I left, that he hit me. My voice still trembles. This is the edge, the jaw-dropping ravine of learning about a husband's infidelity. If only I'd spoken up sooner or gone with him on some of his business trips. Why didn't I have the strength to put my foot down long ago when we needed it?

Enough! This is not your failure.

"Well? Answer me."

"Seven . . . months . . ."

"What? Why? How? We . . . we weren't even married! Fuck! Fuck this. I don't want to hear it. How could you do this to me?"

"Izabel, please, you need to come back to me. She meant nothing to me, and I ended it. I'm nothing without you, baby. *You* are the only thing—the only thing—that makes sense in my life. I love you. I love you so much. I know how badly you've been hurt, but things will change. Remember how good we used to be? We were so happy."

There's a brick in my throat, huge and sharp and choking. It's difficult to speak, even to breathe.

"Izabel, say something." His voice is almost a cry.

"You know, for someone who claims to love me so much, you spend an awful lot of time hurting me. And making me cry. There's no excuse for what you've done. You made me believe I somehow deserved it, and to top it off, you have an affair. You're an abuser, Bo. You . . . are . . . an . . . a-abusive . . . husband. Do you understand how fucked up it is that you would have sex with a woman that *meant nothing* to you and then come home and hit me? You hit me. I'd respect you more if you told me you were in love with her. Did you ever love me?"

"I—" he starts.

"No, let me finish. For more than four years, I have loved you *unconditionally*. Literally. You spent so much time chasing your own dreams, you forgot about our dreams. We were supposed to spend the rest of our lives together. Night after night, I imagined what our children would look like, and what kind of dog we would get, and the family trips we would take." I stop and take a heavy breath. I promised myself I would not cry, but the tears flow freely down my face now. My marriage is over. "But you finally broke me. You ripped out my heart and tore it into a million pieces right before my eyes, and I let you. I would've done anything for you! Congratulations!" The last words come out in a strangled, squeaky shriek.

Bo drops his head in his hands and begins to sob. "Izabel, I need you."

"Where were you when *I* needed you? I will not be your punching bag anymore. I *am* going to move out. I'm *gone*, Bo. Call a real estate agent and sell this house. I'll email you with a date when I would like to come back and collect my things. Make arrangements not to be here on that day."

He says nothing, doesn't look up from his hands. I take one final, deadpan scan of my living room: our beautiful cream walls, fancy Parisian artwork in expensive gilded frames, coffee table books with award-winning photography, the little tchotchkes on the ornate mantle— the room once filled with love and devotion. Now it resembles a crematorium of betrayal and deceit. It's easier this time to walk out without looking back.

Half an hour later, I arrive at Natalie's, suitcase in tow. One of her neighbors is on his way out and politely waits to hold the door for me. He doesn't realize what a relief it is not to have to buzz her apartment and wait on the stoop. I am not ready yet to say a single word.

I lightly rap on her door with the limited energy I have and take a deep breath, dreading the impending monsoon of emotions. I can already feel the lump forming at the back of my throat.

The door swings open. "How could you not tell me? Come here." I know her scolding tone is not directed at me.

She pulls me through the door, but gently wraps her arms around my shoulders, trapping mine down to my sides, and hugs me close. I drop my bags to the floor and feel the last bit of adrenaline and energy drain from my limbs.

"I'll fucking kill him." Her whisper hisses through gritted teeth. I cry even harder at her threat. "I'll fucking—" I don't think Natalie has cried since she was fifteen, but here with me, right now, she's sobbing.

She lowers her embrace around my waist and guides me into her living room. She has a makeshift bed set up on the floor made up of duvets and quilts surrounded by throw pillows. I scan the room. She has provided all the necessary break-up material one would require from a best friend in a situation like this. There is a stack of gossip magazines on the side table, two bottles of wine, colorful bags of candies, the largest bottle of Advil I have ever seen, and a big, fluffy, terrycloth robe.

I should laugh because the sentiment is so unlike her, but all I can bring myself to say is, "Oh, Nat."

"Let's lie down. We can talk about it later. When you're ready."

We plop down onto the cushions, I lay my head in her lap, and she strokes my hair until I can't cry anymore. As my whimpering subsides, I sit up and grab one of the wine bottles. "We're going to need to open this. I need a drink. And you need to be drunk. I need you not to be able to hunt him down."

"That bad, huh?"

"Yup."

"All right, then here we go."

And with the pop of the cork, I begin to relive the horrors of the last year. Natalie sits wide-eyed and speechless, covering her ears at times and crying at others. We break only for her to crack out the pint of chocolate-and-peanut-butter ice cream she had stowed in the freezer, and to get the next bottle open. On and on it goes, as though the story won't end until my voice is raspy and the moon is high.

"So what do we do now? Destroy him?" Her voice is determined.

I give her a kind smile. "*We* don't do anything. This one has to be all me, and no, I can't destroy him. I need time to not think about it for a while, then I guess I'll have to find my own lawyer." With nothing left to say, we're finally confronted by our drunkenness and the silence.

"*You*"—there is a hint of a merry twinkle returning to her eye—"need a distraction." She springs to her knees. "Let's go out with Portia and Henry!" She puts her hands together in a begging gesture.

"No, absolutely not." I scowl. "My marital corpse isn't even cold yet, Natalie, please."

"I know, sorry. I just want you to be happy. Seeing you so sad and broken is hard." Her voice is genuinely apologetic. "What are you doing about work? I hope you're going to take time off."

"Mom called for me. I couldn't do it. She made up a story about a mystery illness and said I will be staying with her for a while so she can take care of me."

"Good. You know you can stay here forever if you want to. You're my soul mate, Jones."

"I know." I smile without effort for the first time in days.

For the next two days, we hold vigil on our make-shift bed, maintaining a steady diet of Thai food, wine, and ice cream, watching chick flicks. Every hour or so, I suffer a mini- breakdown, but the recoveries come quicker as Natalie masters her diversion tactics.

By Friday morning, I'm ready to leave my fortress of solitude. I go into the kitchen to grab some freshly brewed coffee.

Natalie is on the phone in her bedroom. She sneaks around the corner with her hands behind her back.

"Hi." Her voice is ultra-sweet.

"Hi," I respond cautiously.

"Um, someone wants to talk to you." She holds her hands in front of her, presenting me with the phone. "Don't be mad at me, okay?" She pushes it into my hand.

"Natalie, what have you done?" I snatch the cell from her hands and bring it to my ear as though it's a ticking time bomb. "Hello?"

"Hi, Jones. It's Henry."

I look at Natalie and give her a vicious scowl. She mouths the word *sorry* and shrugs her shoulders. I turn away from her and head back to my floor bed.

"Hi, Henry. How are you?"

"How are *you*, actually?" His voice is soft and sensitive. "Natalie told me you've had a bit of a rough go this week. I wanted to make sure you're okay."

"Did she now?" I look up and Natalie is standing in

the threshold between the kitchen and living room. I wave her a warning finger to not come near me.

"I called your cell a few times this week, and when I didn't hear back from you, I got in touch with Natalie." There's a bit of an awkward pause. I can tell he's doing the mental math, trying to figure out if he overstepped some invisible boundary. "I'll, um, completely understand if you are not up for talking right now."

"No, it's okay. It's nice to hear your voice again." It's strange, him expressing concern for me. It makes my stomach flutter, makes the fog hanging over me seem to evaporate. I become aware of my cheek pressing into the mouthpiece, a big, show-your-teeth giddy grin.

"I was hoping you'd say that. The reason I was trying to get in touch with you this week is I have found something that might be of interest to you." He pauses and sighs. "And I'd very much like to see you again, but if you're not feeling up to it, I won't be offended if you decline."

The thought of seeing him, though, makes me freeze. Get dressed? Leave the house? Flirt? Isn't that a little tacky? How long is one supposed to mourn a marriage? Wait—do I still have bruises? But if I say no now, will I ever get another opportunity to say yes?

"Jones?"

"Sure, what did you have in mind?"

"I think Natalie and Portia are meeting up at 2Kats for dinner and drinks tonight. We could meet there."

"Not really up for that." My answer is regretful, but honest. No way can I stand in a loud bar right now. Although a distraction would probably be good for me,

I still need some quiet and peace. "Would you . . . You could come here, I guess?"

"Sure." His answer is immediate, without thought, I think. "I won't take up much of your time. How about I come over around eight?"

That means I'll be alone with him. I look at the clock on the wall. It's only eleven a.m. I still have the rest of the day to change my mind.

"Yes, that will be fine. I'll see you then."

"Great. See you later, Jones." The child-like elation in his voice forces a smirk to the side of my mouth.

I don't notice Natalie standing by the edge of the sofa. She must have snuck her way back into the room. "Well, what did he say?"

"He has something I need to see." My response is detached.

"I'll bet he does." She wiggles her eyebrows at me.

"Natalie . . . Ew!" I scoff.

"You're right, that was totally out of line. So ew. Uber ew. So, when are you seeing him?"

"Tonight. Here."

"He's coming here? When?"

"While you're out with Portia."

Natalie jumps around with excitement. She looks at the clock, then looks back at me. "Holy shit! What are we waiting for then? Let's get you primped."

"Primped? That is *not* what tonight's about."

"Fine. But please, for the love of Christ, at least take a shower. You stink and look like a wet dog. You know I say that out of love." She cocks her head to the side and flashes me a mocking grin.

I shoot her a dirty look and grab a strand of my hair

to examine it. I lift my arm and smell my pit.

"Fine, you win. Primp me."

She claps her hands animatedly like she has just won a line at bingo. "Grab your stuff. We've got to leave the house."

"What? Why?"

"I'm taking you to the water spa for a circuit and an all-over body scrub. Trust me, it feels ah-mazing!"

□ □ □

When I walk out of the scrub room, Natalie is waiting for me on one of the lounge chairs, drinking a green-ish-brown shake. "So, how was it?"

"Well, I feel a little violated now that the nice Filipi-no lady knows me intimately. She scrubbed and waxed me in places I didn't even know existed. But other than that, surprisingly, I feel much better."

"Good. Now let's get you blown before you get blown." She mimes an obscene gesture.

"Seriously? You're killing me." At least today I find her vulgarity marginally amusing.

"Jones, that man is so fucking hot, and he's crazy about you. Don't tell me you haven't thought about it." Her urging evokes a flurry of emotions.

"Yes! He's as hot as the sun, but that doesn't change the whole divorcing-victimized aura I've got going on. And . . . I'm not sure I am quite . . . ready yet. I'm exhausted, and my mind has been deeply hijacked. And . . . I'm still kind of . . . sore." The last couple words are like needles in my throat.

Natalie's eyes swell with tears. "Jones, I'm—I'm so—"

I pull her into a comforting hug. "It's okay, Nat. I know. Come on, let's go get blown." She giggle-cries into the shoulder of my spa robe.

□ □ □

Back at the loft, Nat is putting the finishing touches on her outfit by accessorizing with a faux-fur vest with denim sleeves and the biggest diamond-encrusted skull ring I have ever seen.

A little overkill, but that's Nat. I, on the other hand, have opted for my skinny jeans, a white button blouse, and my UGGs. An intentionally relaxed, un-sexy ensemble.

I've put away my makeshift bed and tidied the place. Natalie is messy on the best of days, but having me here, helpless, to take care of the last few days has taken her aversion to cleaning to a whole new level.

She comes twirling into the room. "How do I look?"

"Gorgeous as usual, *darling*."

"Good, 'cause that's what I was going for. Do me a favor though, retire the Zsa Zsa." She sticks her finger in her mouth, pretending to gag.

Jeez, I didn't think it was that bad.

"Okay, as you know, we are stocked with prosecco. There are a couple of reds in the cabinet and some hard stuff in the freezer. Don't wait up. Portia and I are raving tonight, so we won't be back until dawn."

"That's fine. It will be a quiet night here. I can't imagine Henry will need to be here for more than an hour or so." I look down at my magazine and pretend to flip the pages to avoid eye contact with her.

"Whatever turns your crank, Jones. Now, come gimme a kiss goodbye."

I go over to her and she extends her cheek for me to kiss. She smacks my ass then is out the door like the Tasmanian devil.

Where does that girl get all that energy from? I'm exhausted watching her.

16

At 7:55 p.m., the buzzer goes off. My stomach begins a rhythmical routine of backflips and somersaults. I press the intercom button. "Hello?"

"Hi, it's Henry."

"I'll buzz you up." I take a long sip of my prosecco as I hold down the button.

A few minutes later, there is a knock. I open it right away. Dammit, now it looks like I was waiting.

"Hi."

"Hi. Come in. Please." I stand to the side, holding the door for him to enter.

He nervously kisses my cheek. "Nice to see you again."

"You too. Can I take your jacket?" My voice is a little too high.

"Sure." He slides it off his shoulders, then down his arms, exposing his perfectly toned biceps. He looks better than I remembered. His jeans are tight in all the right places and his gray V-neck T-shirt clings to his defined chest.

I take his jacket and turn to hang it in the front closet, but not before I steal a quick sniff.

Mmm, it smells like vanilla and clove. My body tingles with unexpected delight. It triggers a happy memory from my first PLR session.

"It's cigar."

"What?" I fling my head around to find him watching me. My cheeks heat from the embarrassment of being caught.

"The smell. It's cigar. That was my grandfather's jacket. He always had a cigar tucked in the inside pocket."

"Oh." I clear my throat. "Can I get you a drink?" I hastily scoop up my own glass and take another desperate sip.

"I'll have whatever you're having."

"Okey dokey. Have a seat, I'll be right back." Jeez, who am I, June fricking Cleaver?

The wine bubbles over the top as I pour his glass with a shaky hand. *Shit! Why am I so nervous?* I quickly wipe up the mess, grab his glass and the bottle, and head back into the living room.

Henry is looking at some photos on the wall. He points to one of them. "I can't picture Natalie with long hair. Who's the girl with her?" he asks.

I smirk. "That's me. That was my white-blonde blunt phase, before . . ." I look down at the floor, studying the little tear on the toe of my UGG. "Anyway, that doesn't matter." I hand him his glass.

"Hmm . . . I like it. Not that you don't look— I mean, you look beautiful now too," he stumbles, trying to find his words.

I laugh. "It's okay, no need to explain. I do kind of miss that hair sometimes." I place the bottle on the table by the picture wall and pick up my drink. I face Henry and raise my hand to him. "Well, cheers."

"Cheers." He stares into my eyes.

We sip our drinks with our gazes locked. When I pull the glass away, I inadvertently lick my lips. He smiles and I realize what I've done. I quickly avert my eyes and try to compose myself.

"Um, why don't we sit down?" I suggest.

His beauty is so distracting, it literally makes it hard to focus.

Hastily, I tip back the rest of my glass, reach for the bottle, and fill it again. I'm acutely aware of those mesmerizing eyes watching my every move. This will be my third glass. I'd better slow down.

Henry sits first. I follow, deliberately leaving a cushion's distance between us. The space feels fluid and charged, as though the hairs on my arms can count the millimeters between our bodies.

For a moment, we're quiet, and I have nowhere to rest my gaze, nothing but the stem of the glass to keep my hands busy.

Henry sits back and gets comfortable, draping one arm along the back of the sofa. "This is a nice place. I've always liked loft-style condos. Her windows are fantastic. The view of the water must be spectacular in the day. How long has Natalie lived here?"

"She's been here a couple of years now. It was an impulse buy. I was surprised, to tell you the truth. She's always been a bit of a transient. Making a commitment like this was so . . . out of character for her. It's such a magnificent space. My favorite spot to sit is right over there." I point to a little platform extension halfway up the exposed staircase. "There's almost a panoramic view. At night, the shine from the city reflects off the water. It's so serene. I could watch it for hours."

"I could too," Henry says, snapping me out of my daydream. His gaze is fixed on me. A nervous flutter runs through me. I concentrate on topping up his glass.

"Will you be staying here long?" he asks.

I look down into the tiny golden sea of sparkling bubbles. "I really don't know. I have a few things to sort out first." He must notice my voice, my tone. I don't fault him for asking, though. He has no idea what has happened to me.

"I don't mean to pry. I don't know what happened, but if you need . . . anything, or you want to talk about it . . ." I detect a glimpse of irritation as he eyes the faded bruise and cut on my cheek I attempted to cover with makeup.

"Thank you. That's very kind. It's a long story, and I just don't have the energy for it right now. I'm sorry." I drop my chin and atone for my reluctance to explain.

Henry shifts on the couch, closing the distance between us. He gently cups my chin in his hand and lifts my head to meet his gaze again. "Hey. You have no reason to apologize."

He rubs my shoulder in an effort to comfort me. The all-too-familiar lightning bolt of energy from his touch is seizing. I close my eyes and hold my breath. My eyes spring open when he moves his hand to the nape of my neck. And we're content to just sit there, touching like that, in the stillness.

Visions of our kiss race through my mind. I can still feel his thick hair between my fingers, his warm lips on mine, our hips swaying, our bones pushed up against one another . . . My cell phone's bleating breaks the spell. He drops his hand from my neck and slides back to his cushion.

"I should check that." I fumble with my purse, mumbling something about how she has impeccably bad timing. Once retrieved, I look at the screen and grin.

"Everything okay?" Henry asks.

"Yes. It's Natalie, always the mama hen, checking in on us."

"I hadn't noticed." He laughs.

I'm thankful for the interruption. I need to concentrate on the reason he is here and stop daydreaming. "You mentioned on the phone that you have something for me to see."

He nods and takes a big gulp of his drink before placing the glass on the table behind us. "While I was sorting through some of my grandfather's files, I came across this envelope. I opened it to make sure it didn't contain any legal documents that I might need for his estate." He extracts a thin, faded envelope from his backpack and passes it to me.

"Why are you giving this to me?"

"It's something you need to read, Jones."

The room has shifted. The weight of what he doesn't say presses in on me, but I know it would be no good to question him. So, without hesitation, I lift the broken seal and pull out the content. It is a piece of faded, gritty white paper folded in three, torn around the edges. Gingerly, I unfold the paper to find a few paragraphs of smudged, fountain pen cursive.

My dearest Eve . . .

I gasp and look up at him. His lips are a tight, grim line. "Is this what I think it is?" It's as though a thousand silvery cool brush strokes are pattering over my body. The tiny hairs on my arms stand on end, and my hands begin to tremble. Whispering, I begin to read aloud.

Words cannot begin to explain the pain I felt leaving you after that final, glorious night we spent together. When I first arrived in Detroit, I was merely looking for a distraction. Then I laid eyes on you, a perfect muse, moving about in a world of shadows. You, with your bright spirit and pristine beauty, brought clarity to my broken mind and enraptured my bitter heart. The short time we spent together was the best in my life.

I pray you will understand I had no choice but to follow the path my family had elected for me. Every day I live with regret I did not come back to you, if not to stay, then to give you the respectful farewell you deserved. The thought I may have caused you grief or anguish is a tarnish on my character and a blight on my soul. You see, the man who follows a path laid out for him by others is a craven; the artist who quits his muse is a fool and a peasant both; but the Odysseus who never returns to his Penelope is a lonely vagabond all the rest of his days.

You will be . . .

Forever in my heart . . .

Forever in my soul . . . Forever in my thoughts . . .

You will be my Forever Eve.

Charlie Rudolph

A single tear slides down my cheek and drips off my chin onto the letter, smudging the ink above Charlie's name. Gently, I place the letter down so I can rub my temples.

"Why didn't he send it? They could've had a life together. It's not fair. She died never knowing how much he truly loved her. I saw what her life was like . . . after he left. She never even had a chance for happiness."

Henry strokes my arm. "I don't know why things turned out the way they did. I wish I could ask him, but I can't."

For a few minutes, we sit there, processing. I always tell my patients when they receive difficult information, they need to take deep breaths, let it sink in, not try to resolve everything at once. But my mind is racing. What does it all mean? Why didn't he go back? Does it even matter, all this tragedy that's dead and buried?

Why does it hurt me so?

Then Henry is near me. He moves his hand up to my cheek and caresses me with the backs of his fingers. He cups my face in his palms and uses his thumbs to brush away silent tears I hadn't realized were flowing. His radiant, green eyes entrance me.

"I don't know why my grandfather let her go. Why he'd choose to live with regret instead of joy. But I met *you*."

I lean my head into his touch. His hand is soft and warm, but a cold chill runs through me, making all the little hairs on both arms come to attention and my nipples harden. I turn my head until his fingers rest on my lips. My breathing begins to accelerate from . . .

I'm not sure what. Excitement, nerves, desire. It's like my body is responding to something I don't fully understand.

He closes his eyes briefly and inhales. "Jones—"

"It's okay. I need this, Henry." It seems like an eternity since I've felt so much love and passion. I lean back against the armrest of the sofa and he follows forward, kneeling just above me.

I guide his hand down my neck to my chest, stopping over my heart. I skim his palm over my breasts, and pleasure shoots down my sides. I nod an approval, and he lifts his other hand to join the exploration.

He stops and rests his forehead on mine. "Are you sure?"

I clasp my hands around the back of his neck and gently massage my thumbs behind his ears. "I've never been as sure of anything." I pull his lips to mine.

This time, there is no hesitation from either of us. We explore each other's mouths, and my legs fall open. He nestles in between so I can feel his weight on me. My hands travel down his tight back and up underneath the hem of his shirt. I delicately drag my nails across his skin, making him gasp and moan deep into my mouth. I push my hips off the sofa and rub his growing erection. He pushes forward and grinds on the crotch seam of my jeans, and we move together like crazed, desperate animals.

"Oh yes!" I blurt out and bite down on his lip.

He pulls away, leaving me panting. I wish my clothes would sear right off my skin, expose me, get his skin on my skin, his member inside me. He squeezes harder on my right breast and his open, primal mouth licks and kisses down my throat. We continue to grind—my body can't stop. I don't have time to wriggle out of my jeans. I just have to keep moving against him, making that friction. I could come right now, but I want to savor this feeling, so erotic and carnal.

He stops at the top button of my blouse and grabs it between his teeth. He bites down and tugs, snapping the string free. Henry looks up at me through his gorgeous, lush lashes and grins, displaying the button between his teeth like a playful cat that has just trapped a mouse. He puffs the button onto the floor and moves on to the next, repeating the same slow taunting. I squirm under his weight in search of more friction and manage another thrust.

We've reached his brink. He grabs the new opening of my blouse and rips the rest of the buttons, scattering them all.

"I wanted to go slow, but—I can't wait anymore." He is poised over me with his arms on either side of my head, resting on the end of the sofa. "I want to ravage every inch of you."

I toss my shirt and my bra aside, and his eyes widen with appreciation at the sight of my bare breasts, which are almost aching for him to lick and kiss.

"You are so beautiful, Jones."

Arching my back, I invite him—no, beg him—to go on. His lips are warm over my hard, cold nipples. He twirls his tongue around one, gently tugs at it with his teeth, then devotes himself to the other.

The moans escaping my lips are unrestrainable. "Ohh! I want you. I want you inside me."

I slide my hands down his back and pull the hem of his shirt up over his head, again scratching my nails into his skin on the journey up. We both race to remove our pants. I wiggle mine down past my hips, at the same time fumbling with his belt and button. I can't get them off fast enough. Henry tugs them down, inside-out, past my knees. He rips off my boots and tosses them, pulling off my jeans while shimmying out of his.

Now we're both completely naked. Then ... there it is right in front of me in all its glory: Henry's tremendously erect penis. *Oh my God, of course it's as beautiful as he is.* It looks ... delicious. It's the kind of dilemma of wanting it in my mouth while also wanting it in me that gives me pause. Without thinking, I blush and cover my eyes.

"What's wrong?" he asks, panting.

My eyes still covered, I shake my head. "It's just been so long since I've seen another one."

"We can stop if you want. Really, it's—"

"Are you kidding? I want this. I want *you*." I uncover my eyes and take hold of his more-than-considerable appendage and lightly tickle the tips of my fingers up and down his shaft.

Henry's eyes dim, and he grunts as I tighten my grip, tugging ever so gently for him to come closer. He leans forward, kissing me, bringing his body closer, closer ... I squeeze his cock harder and jut my hips upward, rubbing his tip over my own arousal.

"Fuck. You are so ready."

I throw my free hand over the sofa to the buffet table on the other side and rummage through the glass bowl filled with keys and mail and the condom Natalie put there before she went out. *You never know, Jones*, she'd lectured.

"I'm offended that you assumed I was a sure thing." He winks.

I roll my eyes and giggle. "It's not mine. Nat— Why are we talking about this? Put it on. Now!"

He tears the package and rolls the condom on. With one hand resting beside my head and the other on his erection, he copies my earlier glide, rubbing his tip up and down my moisture, and then he stops at my aching, hungry opening. He rests his forehead on mine and whispers, "Ready?"

"Yes," I answer breathlessly.

Henry slides into me at an ultra-slow pace. I can feel every inch of him as he fills me. He stills and takes a deep, responsive breath. Slowly withdrawing, he then rubs his tip around my clitoris, making my toes curl.

"Make love to me, please," I beg.

Henry kisses my lips tenderly. He enters me again but doesn't stop this time. Increasing his rhythm by just a notch, I join in and wrap my legs around his hips. The contour of our bodies fit together as one, and I push him deeper into me with my heels. We breathe in unison, matching grunt for groan. Given our foreplay, I don't think we have a chance of lasting much longer. I feel the building sensation of desire that has been absent for so long. He hits my sweet spot with every thrust.

I dig my nails into the contracting muscles of his sculpted buttocks, causing him to slam into me harder, and I detonate around him. Every cell in my body explodes from immaculate pleasure. I buck up onto him savagely, half-screaming, half-wailing for one gloriously endless moment as he continues pounding me. I feel his full weight on top of me, and with one final push, he shudders, and a roar escapes from the back of his throat. He collapses and buries his face in my neck, and we greedily gulp the humid air.

"Wow. That was amazing," he says.

"It wasn't bad, I guess." I giggle and squeeze his butt.

"Not bad, you say? I'll have to do better next time." He rewards me with a quick thrust that makes my insides quiver.

"We'll have to find another condom if we're going to continue our little liaison." He slowly pulls out, leaving me wanting.

"Trust me, there is nothing little about your *liaison*." I blush and point down to his still- erect penis.

He smiles and brushes a few stray locks of hair from my eyes. "Let's go get some food. I'm starving. I'm sure we can find a pack of condoms, or ten, on our travels." He gives me a wolfish grin.

I look up at him and all of his perfection, his Adonis body towering over me. I *should* reflect on how I feel about our lovemaking, incredible though it was. Should I feel ashamed or guilty? Should I let it happen again? Was that how Eve and Charlie felt?

I exhale. *I. Feel. Free.* Completely resolved and satisfied with my internal interrogation. "Sounds like a great plan."

17

Still tingling from our tryst, we quickly put ourselves together and burst into the cool November evening. We walk hand in hand in a glorious comfortable silence in no particular direction in search of food.

I steal a glimpse of his face. The lights from the street glow off his perfect complexion. If time were to stop at this moment, my last memory would be of me lying skin to skin in Henry's arms while he caressed my hair. *You are so beautiful*, he whispered.

He stops suddenly and pulls me into an embrace. His lips are on mine. Our tongues are hot kindling against the chill in the air. They tangle without urgency now, two dancers who ace the choreography. My hands are tucked into the back pockets of Henry's jeans for shelter, holding him tight to me for warmth.

"We may freeze to death before we get anything to eat if we keep stopping to kiss."

"It's entirely your fault, you know. You've unleashed . . . a . . . monster!" I drag my tongue under his chin and squeeze his butt.

"I happily take credit for that, Jones. Now, let's get some food."

I stick out my bottom lip and give him a pouty face. "Okay, what do you feel like eating?" I finally concede and pull away.

"Thai?"

Shaking my head at his suggestion, I cover my mouth to stifle the laughing snort sound I just made. My reaction to his simple question was a little dramatic, but I'm in a happy place, and discussing my post-trauma meal isn't necessary right now.

"Okay, Kiss Monster, I'm at your mercy. This is your town."

"And I have just the perfect place." I take hold of his hand.

"You're freezing! Let me warm you up." He envelopes both my hands in his, then creates a little hole between them. He places his lips over it and blows warm air through my fingers.

Where did this man come from? His every move is scripted in some romance novel somewhere. I'm sure of it.

Please don't let me be in a regression. Wherever he's come from, whatever universe we're in, I'm enjoying every nuance of this parallel life I seem to have dropped into tonight.

"There. That's better." His green eyes twinkle under the streetlamps.

"Let's cab it from here. It's a little far. Any other time, I wouldn't mind the leisurely stroll along the waterfront with a wonderful gentleman, but we need to hit a drugstore too." I look at him innocently and bat my eyelashes.

"Taxi!" His arm shoots in the air, and I smile at the urgency in his voice and the comedy in his face.

A taxi pulls up to the curb and we climb inside. "West Harrison in the South Canal loop, please," I tell the driver.

Once we're settled in the back seat, Henry takes my chin in his hand and turns my head to face him. He places a chaste kiss on my lips.

"I thought we weren't kissing anymore," I tease.

"Can't keep my hands off you. Plus, we are in transit, so the rule hardly applies now," he quips with a slow, exaggerated wink.

The cab pulls up in front of the restaurant. I don't give Henry the opportunity to pay, handing the driver more than enough to cover the fare and tip. Impressed with my stealth move, I hop out of the car and extend my hand for Henry to follow.

"You are aware the gentleman is supposed to pay while on a date, aren't you?" He looks almost offended.

"I think we omitted the date formalities about an hour ago by starting the evening off naked and in the throes of passion."

"Good point." He chuckles. "But I *am* paying for dinner."

I agree with a courtly smile. "Hope you like Italian. This place is old school. The menu is whatever the chef has decided to make today. It will be the best thing you'll ever eat."

We follow the bubbly hostess toward the back of the dim, romantic restaurant.

Everywhere I glance, the patrons are couples holding hands, their conversations low as if reciting secret love poems to the cadence of the soft piano that's playing in the background. It's familiar, something pretty that makes my heart flit. I squeeze my arm tighter around Henry's and release a content sigh.

"*Clair de Lune.*"

"What did you say, Henry?"

"This is my favorite piece by Debussy. My grandfather used to play it."

"Hmm."

"Jones?"

"I've . . . heard it before."

"Yeah, it's a pretty famous piece."

"No, I mean, I heard it . . . as Eve. In the regression."

His slightly stunned face slowly stretches into a smile. "See? Another sign from Charlie. I don't know how he knew, Jones, but this—you and I—is kismet."

I'm just pondering the . . . the *predestined* nature of it all when the hostess's voice interrupts my thoughts. "Can I start you with some drinks while you wait?"

I look over at Henry. "I'd love a beer, actually. They have great stuff on tap here."

"Beer works for me too."

"Two Matildas, please."

"Right away. I'll let your server know." She smiles and retreats.

"So, to continue with our most unconventional date, tell me about Izabel Jones." He reaches across the table and locks his fingers with mine.

"Why do you call me by my full name?"

A reminiscent grin curls up the corners of his mouth. "I like the way it rolls off my tongue."

My cheeks flush with warmth from the blatant innuendo. "Do you now? Well, Henry Rudolph, I think you are a bit of a perv." I scratch his palm with my index finger.

"At this rate, we won't get to order." He reaches under the table with his free hand and adjusts himself.

Thank goodness, the waitress arrives with our beer, and we both have to behave like adults in public again.

"Have you decided what you'd like?" Henry returns the palm scratch. I give him a playful kick under the table.

"Yes," I manage to answer as I look at him. "Are you good if I order for both of us?" He smiles.

"Please do."

"We'll have the margarita pizza and the spaghetti bolognese. Oh, and can we get some of that yummy crusty bread with the dip too?"

The waitress scribbles the order on the coil pad. "Great choice."

I take a gulp of my beer and look over at Henry. He's sporting the biggest grin. "What?" I look down at my shirt with fear I've spilled down the front of me.

"You!"

"Me what?"

"You're not a salad girl." He grins even bigger.

I let out a nervous laugh. "Let's just say I'm not a salad girl anymore." He squeezes my hand and gives me an understanding look.

"You were going to tell me more about yourself. I promise to behave this time." He holds up his right hand, crossing his index finger over his middle one.

"It's not that interesting, really. I grew up in Milwaukee, and of course, you know all about Natalie. My mom raised me alone." I bypass the details of that part. "Natalie and I have been best friends since elementary school. Um, what else?"

I tap my fingers against my chin and look off into memories of my life.

"I went to UChicago. Full scholarship, thankfully. According to Nat, I missed out on all the high school fun because I always had my nose stuck in books, but my mom was always working two jobs, so it was a real blessing. I completed my Masters in Behavioral Psychology back in April, and now I work for Dr. Kennedy analyzing habitual behaviors, and the rest . . ." I take a long pause and a deep breath. "And the rest is history."

I grimace a little, hoping the Bo-shaped absence looks to Henry like a small hole, rather than the crater it is. His smile seems to say, *What elephant? I'll ignore it if you will.* I've never felt more grateful for a smile.

"Have you considered going back for your PhD?"

"That's always been the plan, but . . . now I'm not sure what the future holds for me. One day maybe. And that's my life in a nutshell."

I raise my glass and take a sip of beer. Suddenly, I feel the need to explain to him, or maybe to myself. My life shouldn't be *in a nutshell*. These last few turbulent days have left me soul-searching for something more, something life defining.

"Henry, I have always led a scheduled life. I hit every milestone I was supposed to, exactly when I was supposed to. Until now. Everything's a little . . . off kilter today. And I kind of like it, but I'm also not sure about . . . a lot of things."

"Welcome to real life, Jones, where the only milestones you have to hit are the ones you want to hit. One of the perks of being a citizen of the Western world in the twenty-first century."

I take another gulp of my beer, trying to avoid eye contact. I am thankful for yet another welcome interruption as our waitress returns with our food, placing the plates in the middle and asking about irrelevant things like fresh grated parmesan and fresh cracked pepper. We say yes to both, but I've somehow switched onto auto-pilot.

Nerves have overcome me. It's not unease. It's something more profound. I hardly know him, but it feels like we've spent a thousand nights like this before. It *feels* like Charlie and Eve paved the path for us. But that also feels like something a crazy woman would say, before her date gets totally freaked out and leaves.

I just want to know . . . Does he feel it too? The question hovers on my lips when Natalie's advice from the gallery night strikes me. *Explore the endless possibilities.* Don't ask. Don't define. Don't cut it off at the knees. Don't pry. Don't pin everything down. Just explore.

Henry takes a big bite of one of the pizza slices. "You weren't kidding," he mumbles inelegantly between the huffing noises he's making to cool his mouth from the scalding hot cheese he's just ingested. "This is the best thing I've ever eaten."

"I know, right?" My manners have also been abandoned. "Okay, my turn. Read me the CV of your life."

He holds up a finger and finishes chewing. "I'm a structural engineer, which is pretty cool. My firm is international, so I've been fortunate to travel a lot."

"That's so cool. I've never been past the Great Lakes." I bite down on a piece of crusty bread.

"So cool is right. Traveling to countries like Dubai and China and Morocco . . . it's really life changing. Hmm, let's see. I have three older brothers, and Portia's the youngest. Being the baby, she was spoiled and is, if you haven't noticed. Our house was controlled chaos all the time. My mom was an actress—theater, not movies—and would be away for weeks at a time, but she somehow managed to keep us all reined in, sort of. One of us—I can't remember who—dubbed her 'The General' one day. We called her that in secret for about, I don't know, two weeks, before she caught wind of it and loved it. So nowadays, that's how we all lovingly refer to her.

Whether she was home or away we always had our lists, homework, chores, you know. We griped as kids, but we are thankful as adults. You should see me make a bed. You could bounce a coin off it." He winks and takes another big bite before continuing.

"Dad's a philosophy professor at NYU. He is much less dramatic than my mother. He's very level-headed. My oldest brother is my grandfather's namesake, but he likes us to call him Chuck. He's a doctor in Boston. He and his wife Sophia have pre-teen triplet girls. They're sweet, but I don't envy him, seriously. His house is bursting at the seams with hormones, cell phones, and locked bathroom doors."

I could listen to him all night. I twirl the spaghetti onto my fork and pop it into his mouth, interrupting him mid-sentence.

He chews, then nods. "Mmm, that is tasty. I must be boring you will all this family talk."

"Not at all. I'm an only child. I'm fascinated by the

sibling dynamic." I perch my elbows on the table and lean forward with interest.

"Okay. William, brother number two, and his long-time girlfriend live in Manhattan. They both deal in high-end real estate. He used to be quite the . . . player, 'til he met Monica. I don't think they'll ever have kids."

He pauses to eat, and I can see the thinking going on behind his eyes. He's picturing them, remembering things I can't know, seeing their faces, replaying memories. The love is stitched across his face like needle-point, but his brow furrows a little as he speaks again.

"Then there's Thomas. He's a bit of a drifter. Good guy, don't get me wrong, but he's just lost. His wife was killed in a car crash and, understandably, he never recovered. One day, he donated most of his stuff, sold a few of the bigger things for some extra cash, then hopped on a plane to I-don't-know-where. He checks in with us every few months from a different part of the world. It broke my mom's heart. I don't really get it, but I know enough to understand that he's got to do his own thing, you know?"

"I'm so sorry."

He smiles gently. "Thanks. It was tough. She was a beautiful person. And it was worse to see him so angry and bitter. And to not be able to do anything. I'd be having a great day at work, go out for beers with my friends afterward, and then I'd see a text from him, and I'd know he was alone. Wallowing. It makes you feel like shit. That life has moved on, that you dared to be happy, and they've just been . . . left behind. Like I had the audacity to be laughing in a bar when my brother's whole existence was in shambles. Of course, he never wanted me to feel that way, but he's my brother. It was incredibly difficult to see him so despondent and not be able to do a damn thing, but I also didn't want to be angry or bitter."

He takes a slow, measured sip of his beer, and I look across the restaurant for a moment, pretending to be intrigued by something happening in the distance.

"But just like Abe Lincoln said, 'In the end it's not the years in your life that count, it's the life in your years.' Great first date talk, eh? Sorry, didn't mean to get so heavy."

"Don't apologize. I should thank you for sharing this part of your life with me."

He's humble and vulnerable. My heartache melts away, and in its place grows yearning. Talking is no longer an option. I need to feel his body again, his beautiful skin against mine. I want to be audacious.

Rising from my seat, I lean across our small table and kiss his neck below his ear then take his earlobe in my mouth for a little nibble. "I want you . . ." I exhale a low pant into his ear. "*Now.*" His breath hitches, and he shivers. I sit back in my seat. "I think I need one more taste though." I run my index finger along the edge of the pasta plate, smearing the red sauce. Staring across the table at Henry with seductive eyes, I slide my finger into my mouth. With a deliberately slow pull, I suck the sauce from my finger and pop it out of my mouth with a grin.

Henry shifts in his chair and flags the waitress. "Could we get the check, please?" The crack in his voice makes me giggle. *Mission accomplished.*

□ □ □

We make it back to the loft in record time, even after the detour to the drugstore. It took all of our willpower not to strip each other on the way. Luckily, we didn't bump into any of the neighbors, not that I would've noticed.

I fling the door closed behind us and Henry hoists my legs up around his hips. He leans into me against the back of the door and ravages my neck with his teeth. I feel his raging erection press between my legs.

"Oh God, I . . ." I can't even complete my sentence.

He turns and carries me across the room without unlocking our lips. Walking blind, he bumps into the dining table then the chair.

I tighten my grip around his neck until he finds an open space. Without loosening our embrace, he effortlessly lays me on the floor, pulls off my shirt then his, and tosses them to the side.

"You are so beautiful." He trails kisses down my neck and onto my breasts.

He reaches behind me and unhooks my bra, freeing my waiting nipples. He tenderly kisses each one but doesn't stop there. He continues his trail down my stomach and tugs at my zipper with his teeth. The button of my jeans had already been taken care of in the hallway. I feel his nails prickle my skin as he inches my jeans and panties down my legs. My hips are up, off the floor, helping him discard my jeans in the same fashion as my shirt.

I tense as he runs his fingertips up the inside of my thighs. I raise my hips farther off the ground, offering myself to his puckered mouth. He glides his warm tongue across my swollen lips and blows softly on my clitoris.

Little by little, he slides a finger inside of me, then a second one. I release a slow whine and drive my hips higher, forcing his fingers deeper. He penetrates me expertly, twisting and turning, stroking my inner walls on all sides.

I peek between my knees and catch his green-eyed gaze—like kerosene on a fire. I run my fingers through his hair and tug harder with every lap of his tongue. He synchronously moves his finger and tongue in and out of me, over and over, increasing his momentum. *Please, never end. Never end.* In and out, in and out, in and out, again and again. The tingling pinch building in my belly makes me twitch and squirm. I begin to gyrate, matching his rhythm.

I moan loudly. My climax is coming. Henry breaks and looks up at me with hooded eyes.

He licks his lips. "You are dripping down my finger. Come in my mouth, baby. I want to taste you."

I've lost all cognizance of my surroundings. Every nerve ending in my body is concentrated on that one spot, deep in my belly, that is ready to burst. Henry removes his finger and tightens his grip around my hips, limiting my movement. He continues to nibble and bite and lick until I can no longer hold back.

"Henry, I'm coming!" I shatter around his tongue as he drinks me in. "Let it go, baby."

He ignores my wails to stop and inserts a finger again, hitting my tender erogenous zone and inducing a plentiful flow of orgasmic juice. I keep riding it out, pushing onto him, feeling it through every nerve. Finally, he relents. I lie tranquil and purring, wiping mist from my eyes.

He sits back on his heels and rubs inside my thighs again, attempting to soothe my intermittent convulsions. "Mmm," he grunts. "I have to amend my earlier statement from this evening. You by far are the best thing I've ever tasted."

He rolls his body back up me until his glistening lips are on mine. He plunges his tongue deep into my mouth, urging me to relish my climax.

"Taste how delicious you are."

I accept his offering hungrily and twist my tongue onto his. "Wow, what was that?" I wheeze.

"That is what you call letting go completely." He kisses the tip of my nose. "Did you enjoy it?"

"Enjoy it?" I pant, still trying to catch up with my breathing. "I'm not even sure what just happened to me, but I'd like to return the favor."

I flip out from underneath him and straddle his mid-section. I flinch from the sensitivity still radiating from me. I lean forward and bite one of his nipples. He inhales audibly and pushes my hips farther down.

We are beyond seduction at this point. It is animalistic. We need to feed off each other. I want him in my mouth. I yank his pants below his knees, followed by his boxers, and crawl toward his enormous cock. I toss my hair over my shoulder so he has a clear view of my pending performance. He raises himself onto his elbows, watching me. I take him in both hands and studiously lick his head a few times. He brings his hand up to my head and grabs hold of the long strands of hair down my side, giving me a gentle tug of gratification. I lower my mouth on to him with a deep breath. I have to loosen my jaw to accommodate his girth and length.

A few test strokes later, I am effortlessly pulling him to the back of my throat, tasting the mixture of his musk and his flesh, feeling his pulse against my tongue. His groans spark me. I pull back up lightly, grazing my teeth along his shaft.

He grips my shoulders and pulls me up. "I want to be inside you when I come."

I reach for the condom and roll it on urgently. I straddle him again and steady myself. With one hand, I guide him into me, slowly, teasingly, inch by magnificent inch. Just when he starts to smile, I slow down even more, feeling the width of him stretching me.

My hips begin to move back and forth. He squeezes my ass, assisting my rhythm, stirring me faster up and down onto him. Now we're really moving, thrusting madly in unison, me riding him harder and faster, him pushing the full length of himself deep into me again and again. His thrusts are so powerful, the sensation hijacks my body, provoking me to cry out and clench around him. He counter-attacks with another thrust, lifting me clear off the ground and pushing his head so far into me he hits my sweet spot and sends me spiraling out of control. I unleash my orgasm onto him, wildly rocking back and forth while he tries to pull me down onto the base of his shaft, growling foul things as he comes.

He wraps his arms around my shoulders after I buckle on top of him. We are drenched in sweat, panting, and gloriously sore. "You are incredible. Where have you been all my life?"

I reach up onto the sofa and pull the throw blanket down, covering us. With my head tucked under his arm, I close my eyes and fade away to the sound of his voice.

"Sleep now, baby. Dream of us."

18

I open my eyes to the tapping toe of an Alexander McQueen in my face. I am in the same position I was in when I fell asleep, but now sunlight fills the room. Henry is still asleep underneath me. I look up to find Natalie staring down at me, nearly doing a happy dance. *Shit.*

I'm never gonna hear the end of this.

"Good morning, sunshine." She breaks into some sort of interpretive dance move as she chimes her greeting to me.

I pull the blanket up over my head and pretend she can't see me.

"I'll be in the kitchen getting coffee when you're ready to grovel." Her heels click away across the hardwood floors.

I remove my blanket and slide to the side so I don't wake Henry. I throw on my oversized sweater and follow her to the kitchen. Natalie leans on the counter, stirring her coffee. She hands me a steaming mug and smiles.

I decide to break the silence first and clear my throat. "So, how was your night?" I look down into my coffee.

"It was good. How about yours? Do anything out of the ordinary?" She smirks and I take another sip, trying to hold back my elated grin.

"So . . . big cock?"

I spit across the room. "Natalie, is nothing sacred to you?"

"Trust me, Jones, there is nothing sacred about mouth banging."

She starts to mime fellatio but is interrupted by Henry, who walks into the kitchen half- naked. He is shirtless and his jeans sag slightly off his hips, revealing the perfect V that leads down to his pubic area. She freezes and turns a shade of red I've never seen before.

She shifts her lewd hand gesture to a salute. "Morning, captain."

I slap my hand over my eyes, not sure if I'm embarrassed by the fact she knows I had sex with this gorgeous man standing half-naked in front of us, or by the fact that he did things to me last night that I have only seen in a movie once, or because at this very moment filth riddles my thoughts as to what I would like to do to him right now on the kitchen counter.

"Good morning, ladies." Henry saunters over to me, leans down, and tenderly kisses my lips. I instantly turn to mush.

"Can I pour some coffee for you?" I ask lovingly.

"Yes, please. And some water, if you wouldn't mind? I seem to be little dehydrated." He winks, making me blush once more. "Where's Portia?" Henry looks around as though on a swivel.

"The wife's grabbing us some croissants. She'll be up in a minute. You know, in case you want to make yourselves decent, you dirt-bags."

Henry doesn't seem fazed by her response. I hand him his beverage and the three of us stand in silence, sipping our coffee. I catch Nat's eye and motion for her to leave.

"Well, I'm going to freshen up." Her voice is a little too obvious. Whatever. At least I got her to leave us alone.

Once she's out of sight, Henry turns to me and wraps me in his arms. He rests his forehead on mine and closes his eyes, sighing contentedly. "Jones, it's hard to describe what you and I have. But it's powerful. And it's real. I want you to know that."

"I feel the same way. It's kind of overwhelming." I close my eyes and draw in his heavenly scent.

He hugs me closer. "Let's go to your favorite spot and drink our coffee. We kind of got sidetracked on the get-to-know-you conversation last night."

I give him a shy smile. "I think I have a new favorite spot." I slide my hands down to his butt and give him a mischievous squeeze.

"Well, aren't you a little temptress?" He lifts me onto the counter, and I wrap my legs around his waist.

"If we keep this up, we'll end up having sex right here on the kitchen counter. I don't think Natalie would appreciate that . . . but then again, she'd proba-bly watch and shout out game plays." He looks at me and we laugh at his accurate hypothesis of her. Laughter quickly turns to something deeper. Our breathing accelerates. I am reminded I'm not wearing anything under my sweater when he leans between my legs and presses his arousal against me.

"Woo." I breathe deep. "You're right. We'd better stop. Come with me." I lead him to the staircase, and we climb halfway up to my platform. Henry sits first, then I climb into his lap.

"Wow! The view is even more spectacular in the daylight. I can see why this is your second-favorite spot."

I wriggle as he pinches my sides. "I told you. Oh, look! I'm always amazed that people still sail this time of year. It must be freezing out there."

The sun glistens off the waves, bouncing into the loft and concentrating on our spot. It feels so warm, like we are enclosed in our own private solarium. I could sit here all day with him, with his arms wrapped tightly around me and not a care in the world.

Natalie ensures that doesn't happen. "Hey, love-birds, I have to go run an errand with Portia. We'll be back in a while. Don't do anything I wouldn't do. Oh yeah, you already did that. Well then, do everything I would do. Hahaha!"

I can't see her from where we sit, but knowing Nat, she has gestured something rude to follow her comment.

"Okay, that'll do. Bye, Nat." I twist my body around just enough to watch her walk out the door.

After the front door closes, we sit in an organic, comfortable silence, watching the reflective rays dance across the water. It would be so easy to fall in love with him. I suspect I may have already.

"Tell me more about Henry Rudolph. I want to hear about your work. I want to hear about your worldly travels. Where you have been? Where do you want to go? Where is your favorite place so far?"

"That's a lot of questions before eight a.m." He laughs. "But I'll try. For you. Ask away."

I lean back against him and get cozy. "Oh, this is going to be fun, like speed dating—one answer for every question. I'll ask a bunch first. Ready?"

"Ready."

"Where did you go to college? First place you ever traveled to? Name of your first girlfriend? First time you had sex? Favorite song?"

"Woah, slow down there." He tickles my sides, making me jump. "Let's see if I can remember them all." Henry pulls me closer to him and leans his chin on my shoulder. "I went to NYU. Traveled to France with my family when I was twelve. First girlfriend was Elizabeth. Sex and Elizabeth—that was an interesting relationship." His little chuckle from the memory vibrates off my shoulder. "*Three Little Birds* is my favorite song."

"Yay. That's mine too." I turn my head and kiss his chin.

"Is there anything else your enquiring mind would like to know, Izabel Jones?"

"Yes, actually. How old are you?"

"Does that really matter at this point in our relationship?"

"No, but I want to know."

"Thirty."

"Okay, last two, for now anyway. Where have you always wanted to travel to? And where is the best place you've visited to date?"

"I've always wanted to go to the Serengeti. And the absolute most life-changing place I've ever traveled to would be Lumbini, Nepal. After Thomas's wife passed, I needed to find perspective in my life. I was so driven by success and money. I didn't have time for anyone. It's the most spectacular place on earth. I discovered a spiritual side I didn't know I had. Watching the Monks and Nepalese people . . . well, it really changes the way you see things. It makes you realize you don't need any stuff. I haven't needed or wanted anything until I met you, Jones."

My heart skips a beat. I tighten his embrace around me and tilt my head back. I raise my lips to his and he offers the most delicate kiss.

He moves his lips to the little scab that has formed on my cheekbone and rests for a few seconds. "I don't want to know about this, do I?" he whispers onto the scab.

I shake my head. "Not yet." I'm not sure if it's because I'm not ready to talk about what happened or if I'm worried what he'll think of me once he knows.

He softly brushes the area with his beautiful mouth as if trying to erase my memory of the painful infliction. Henry lifts my hair and kisses the little indent at the back of my neck, sending shivers down my spine and directly between my legs.

"Jones, you have no idea what you've done to me. I can't keep my hands or my mind off of you." He slides back so I'm sitting on the platform and not his lap. He continues his kisses down the back of my neck and massages my shoulders gently.

"Mmm, that feels so good," I purr.

"You're so tight. Let me make it better for you."

He moves his hands down my arms, massaging down to my fingers, digging his thumbs into the pad of skin in the palm of my hands. I feel his erection growing behind me, but I ignore it for now, luxuriating in his touch. I'm sure I won't be able to ignore it for long, though. I have never had an addictive personality, but I think I've found my gateway drug in Henry.

He works his skillful hands to my thighs. Uncrossing my legs, he lifts my knees up to my chest and hooks his feet around my ankles so I can't straighten them. He gently nips at my earlobe and begins to massage my thighs, starting at my knees then slowly working his way down the insides.

I know exactly where he's going, and elation fills me. This is beyond erotic. I'm totally open and exposed—delivered. I want this man to know every curve of my body. He is my past, my present, and my future. His hand grazes past my clitoris, swollen and raised and waiting. I twitch in anticipation. He teases the lowest point of my inner thighs without touching my sex.

I whimper, trying to invoke his mercy on me. "Touch me, Henry."

"I will." He nibbles the side of my cheek playfully. I push my behind back onto him to add strain to his now full erection.

He bites my earlobe with sensuous challenge. Moving his hands closer together, he massages my outer lips, making me tremble. The delayed gratification is agonizing.

Trailing two fingers up to my clitoris, he begins small, circular motions clockwise, then counter-clockwise, or the reverse, I'm not sure. It just feels so good. I can't straighten my legs for any escape, and when I try and push back onto him, his orgiastic rhythm increases. He pulls at my hair with lustful force, exposing the full surface of my neck, and I willingly comply. His tongue emulates the same circular motions of his fingers, bridging the sensation at either end of my body.

"Oh, Henry, what have you done to me?" I whimper and move my hips to the tempo of his fingers, aiding my waiting release.

"Let it go, baby."

I tense and try to straighten my legs, but he holds me tighter, forcing me to endure and accept my peak. I bite down on his forearm that is wrapped around my chest in hopes of diverting his energy, but he continues his lavish strokes, causing seizures of pleasure until I am a pool of orgasmic nectar. "Oh, oh, oh!"

He unhooks his legs from mine and rubs them as I stretch out, sending residual tremors through my body. I nuzzle into him, my back to his front. He hugs me in close and hums in my ear. "I'd like to share this spot with you forever."

"Mmm, I'd like that. I would also like to make some breakfast for you. Then shower with you and spend the rest of the day in bed making love to you."

With one effortless move, he pulls me back onto his lap. He grabs the nape of my neck and kisses me passionately. Our tongues twirl together with newly discovered love and desire. I feel the vibration of his groan in the back of my throat.

"God, I love you, Jones."

I take his face in my hands and stare deep into his

mesmeric green eyes. There is complete silence in the loft except for our hitched breathing. Nothing else in the world matters right now.

"I love you too, Henry."

He smiles and plants wet kisses all over my face. "That makes me incredibly happy. Now, how about that breakfast?"

We walk hand in hand down the stairs into the kitchen. Henry hops up on the counter beside the fridge. He looks so sexy sitting there cross-legged and shirtless. I can't concentrate on what I need to do. I'm still whirling. *Henry loves me, and I love him.*

I can feel a spot on my ribcage, an old bruise that's been aggravated by all of our wild play. Bo. He isn't gone yet. He'd be furious if he found out . . . *But it's not his business anymore, is it?* Still, I don't want these two worlds to collide. That's baggage Henry shouldn't have to deal with. Distance will help. With Henry back in New York, there'll be no chance of overlap. Wait.

New York? He's three feet from me right now, and that's too far. New York . . . "Hey, baby, I think you've beat that batter to death."

I've spilled pancake batter all over the place. I twirl the spoon in the bowl, and I flick batter onto his chest. I giggle innocently. "Oops, I might have to come clean that off you now."

He jumps off the counter and is beside me in a split second. I hide the spoon behind my back so he can't grab it from me. He pulls me in and tickles me. In his arms is exactly where I want to be, but I wiggle for an escape from his playful assault.

"I'll hand it over, I promise."

He doesn't stop though. He holds me tight with one arm, tickling me with the opposite hand until the spoon clatters to the floor.

He cups my naked butt and tingles spike through my body. I want him again right now on the tile. I wiggle one hand free from his grip and rub the outline of his cock through his jeans. It hardens instantly. I stick my hand down the front of his pants and squeeze him gently in my palm. "I think I can help you with this."

"I know you could help me with this." His mouth finds mine and we are once again tangled in arousal.

I am aware of a faint conversation going on at the front door, but I ignore it as we continue to kiss. But the voices become clearer and more aggressive ... It's—

"What the *fuck's* going on here? Get your fucking hands off my wife!"

I whip my head around. Bo storms in, Natalie and Portia right behind him looking terrified. I instinctively stand in front of Henry, trying to shield him. He moves to get around me, but I shuffle so he can't get by. I feel his rigid upper body flush with my back.

"Bo, what are you doing here?" A heavy combination of fear and rage is driving the pitch in my voice.

"I thought I would come and see if I could bring my wife home and make things work. Who knew she would have turned into a *fucking whore* in such little time?"

Henry lunges forward, but I dig my heels downward and throw my body weight against him, struggling to hold him back. I somehow find the strength to hold him in place.

"And who the fuck are you, you little jumped up piece of shit?" Bo spits.

"Don't answer him." Pushing back against Henry, I widen my stance and plant my feet. I desperately want to turn and look into his eyes to assure him everything will be okay, but I'm afraid if I lose sight of Bo, even for a second, something bad might happen.

"What? You don't get any, so you have to screw another man's wife, is that how it is?"

"Last I checked, a real man doesn't beat his wife." The heat from Henry's growl warms the back of my neck.

"Say that without Izabel in front of you, coward."

"Enough!" My voice is shrill, like broken strings of a violin.

It's hard to breathe. I'm literally frozen with fear. I stare wide-eyed at Portia, hoping she will understand my telepathic pleas. *Move your feet.*

One step, then another, I reluctantly move away from Henry and closer to Bo. His face is purple as he glowers down at me, fists clenched at his sides. I am stricken with panic. This tactic might not turn out the way I plan. I close my hands around Bo's fists and lift his arms around me in an embrace.

"Jones . . ." Hearing Henry say my name makes my body tremble.

With Bo's arms fixed around me, I look over at Henry and hope he can see through what I'm trying to do—that this is the only way he and I can eventually be together. "You don't understand, Henry. He needs me."

A satisfied little smirk flickers on Bo's face.

Portia creeps around us and leans in to whisper in Henry's ear. "We should go."

As they move past us, the look of grief on his face is

enough to render me spineless. I feel like I'm going to faint. It's as if my heart has just been ripped from my chest. But I need to see this through, so I rest my head on Bo's chest and his muscles relax a bit. Silent tears fall from my eyes.

"I am so sorry, Bo."

His arms close around me like a python suffocating his fresh prey.

I begin to sob as I hear the front door close. Poor Henry. He must think the worst. I couldn't have him be witness to the humiliation and degradation that is about to materialize.

Natalie walks back in the room tentatively with a look of shock on her face. "Jones, are you okay?"

I nod. My body defies me, however, and my stomach retches, but I swallow it back. "Give us a minute, Nat." I wave her off.

She squints her eyes and regards Bo with a look of disgust. "I'll be upstairs if you need me."

I nod again.

I pull away from Bo's embrace. I feel sick at the thought of him touching me again. "Izabel, you think you can leave me and jump into bed with the first man you meet? It doesn't work that way. You are my wife, for better or worse." His voice is slack and insolent.

Don't be afraid. I stand tall and wipe the tears from my face. "What would you know about for better or worse? The last time I checked, a husband isn't supposed to beat and rape his wife." I take a step back from him, spread my arms out, and raise my chin. *Bring it.* "Go ahead and hit me, you coward. But don't *ever* refer to me as your wife again."

He raises his fists to his temples, pounding his own head, moaning and raging. "You goddamn fucking—" He throws a punch into the wall, cracking the drywall, swearing again.

"It doesn't matter what you say, Bo. I'm not afraid of you anymore." I prepare myself for a blow, but instead he drops to the floor. He buries his head between his knees and sobs.

His apologies spill out in muffled, choking bursts. "I'm so sor-sorry, Izabel. You have to believe me . . . never meant to hurt you. I don't know how to control this. I need you. Please come back to me, to help me."

I slide down the wall and slouch beside him. "Bo, look at me." My voice is soothing.

The words of wisdom from Henry's story about his sister-in-law's death bring calm and clarity to my thoughts. *I don't want to be filled with hatred and bitterness.* It would be so easy to hate Bo right now, but what good would that do either of us? I can't change what has already been done to me.

He turns to face me, his eyes red and teary.

"We spent over four years together, and most of that time was wonderful. You were my entire existence. But these wounds are too deep. I don't want either of us to hurt anymore, but we can't be together if you want to get better. *I* can't make you get better. You need to rediscover who you are and be happy with yourself again before you can even think about making anyone else happy. I genuinely want that for you."

He sits silent, his eyes now vacant and void of expression. I slide back up the wall. The tables are turned as I stand over him while he cowers. I don't feel powerful at all. I realize how deep his affliction must be and the torment he must have been faced with each time he had me in this position.

"I love you, Izabel."

"I know you do, Bo, but you need to go now." I hold out my hand to help him up off the floor. "I'll walk you to the door."

As we walk hand in hand, the feeling is bittersweet. A part of me will always love the happy memories I have with Bo, but they're just that—memories.

When he leaves, I close the door behind him and lean my back against it for support. My body is numb, but there is no urge to cry. I am emotionally dehydrated. My knees give way and I crumple to the floor. I slide down the door. I am a carcass waiting for my inner vulture to carry me away to feast feverishly on the desolate organ that was my heart.

Natalie has come to sit beside me. She leans back against the door and clasps my hand, twirling her fingers into mine. I give her a squeeze and rest my head on her shoulder. We sit in silence for what seems like hours. Finally, she places my cell phone into my free hand. I scroll through my history and press *call*.

"It's Izabel." My disembodied voice is barely a whisper. "Call me. Please."

"Voice mail?" Natalie asks.

"Yes." I am the puppet waiting for my master to pull at my strings for my next move. "I'm gonna go back to Mom's again tomorrow for a while."

"Okay." She doesn't challenge me.

I twist my legs to the side and push up off the floor. It's like trudging through quicksand to get across the room. Curling up into a ball in the corner of the sofa, I wrap the throw blanket around me. I need the scent of him. I close my eyes and succumb to my exhaustion, slipping into an apathetic coma.

When I wake, I see the sun setting over the water through the picturesque windows of the loft, although I am forsaken by the beauty of the scene. I fight to keep my eyes sealed. I don't want to be exposed to reality. Not yet.

Natalie kneels at the edge of the sofa in front of me and clears my hair away from my face. "Are you hungry?" Her comfort is so heartfelt, but it doesn't help the pain I feel.

I shrug. "Did he call?"

"No, babe. He will though." She strokes my hair again.

I stretch out my legs and move forward, inviting Natalie to crawl in behind me. She delicately complies and pulls me in close.

A tear rolls out of the corner of my eye and slowly trickles across my nose, finding its resting place on my hand cradled under my head. I drift back into my oblivion.

I spend most of the next morning in my spot watching the waves on the water, devoid of all thoughts. I reread Henry's texts over and over.

I'm sorry I couldn't call.

I'll be traveling with work for a while and will be unreachable. Please believe me when I say I am not leaving with any bitterness. xo Forever Henry

My brain refuses to process this situation. My fight-or-flight response has completely abandoned me, and

I make my way back down the stairs and gather up the few contents I have with me to begin the short journey back to Mom's. I need to be away from here—to re-balance. There is no sorrow or fear left in me. I am an abyss of nothingness.

"Do you really have to go?" Natalie weeps, holding my purse hostage.

Seeing her so fragile makes everything much harder for me. But she's shell-shocked. I don't know if she's ever seen rage like that before.

"It's what's best for me. Besides, who better to make me want to come back than my mother?" I give her a weak smile, trying for some levity. "I'll call you when I get there."

"What are you doing about work?"

"I don't know. I'll figure that out tomorrow." She relinquishes my purse sadly.

"Nat, I'm not far, and I'll be back in no time. I have to. Who will look after you if I don't?"

She hugs me close then grabs onto my ass and squeezes tight. I knew my Nat wasn't far away.

19

I allow myself a couple of weeks of nothingness at Mom's before I begin my emotional repair. After all, when hitting rock bottom there's only one direction to go. I figure this once, I don't have to rush. There are no deadlines but mine.

I finally find the courage to call a lawyer to start the divorce proceedings. One of the first official communications I received from Bo's attorney was a veiled request to keep things "hush-hush" so it doesn't tarnish his career. It's enough to make me spit. That's Jack Carmichael talking loud and clear. *I don't care what happened to you. I don't care your heart is broken.*

Keep your pretty mouth shut. I'm sure "Wife Beater for Governor" would attract all kinds of media attention.

I find myself experiencing all the bursts and pangs of a widow. Sometimes rage ripples through me; other times I just feel an immense black-blue sadness. I remember us. Seems like long ago now, being so content, holding hands, and it's still jarring to think of those same hands hurting me. It feels like . . . like I'm crumpled-up foil, tossed in a waste basket, forgotten and irrevocably crushed.

One thing I never expected are the nightmares. I should have known from my years studying psychology I'm a prime candidate for PTSD, but, like everybody I guess, I never thought it would happen to me. I dream of belt buckles and deep, dark crawl spaces, footsteps overhead, but nobody can hear me or lets me out.

I'm satisfied with the one provision I've been able to set now that our communications comprise only of formal documents, legal jargon, and bartering of assets, tangible and intangible. Whether the threat I pose to expose his secret is real or not, Bo has conceded that he will maintain his therapy. I truly want him to get better. He offered to help me financially so I can go back to school, but, bribe or not, I think severing ties is the best decision for both of us. Once we sell the house, I'll have enough money to start my doctorate, if that's what I choose.

I knew there would come a point when I would have to come clean with Dr. Kennedy. A mystery illness is only believable for so long. It also wasn't fair to Mom that she had to screen my calls and continue to lie for me. And quite honestly, I couldn't do it on my own anymore. Dr. Kennedy is a wonderful doctor, and I truly respect his counsel. It only made sense to ask for his help. He understood I couldn't bring myself to make the drive into Chicago. I needed distance from my reality for I didn't know how long.

However, Dr. Kennedy felt it was germane to my healing process to have FaceTime sessions. He believes that facial expressions and body language sometimes say more than actual words. How do you tell a man you highly respect that you've been subject to a heinous crime that you only read about in the newspaper or see on the news? Then follow that up with, "And, oh yeah, I traveled back in time and met my lover's grandfather, who was in love with the girl I was in my past life who happened to be a prostitute" without him thinking that you're bat-shit crazy?

As hesitant as I was to open up to him, eventually I did, and he listened without judgment. He had a theory that while in my hypnotic state I manifested these characters out of desperation. Eve and Charlie's love paralleled what Bo and I had at the beginning of our relationship. This is what I craved to have back in my life.

And the cycle of abuse was a subconscious attempt to justify Bo's behavior. I fought the notion that this would be a lengthy process, but Dr. Kennedy is a brilliant therapist and I trust his guidance and healing methods.

Mom has been really supportive and understanding too. I feel bad about the comment I made to Nat that Mom will be what drives me back to Chicago. I will need to face the real world again soon and find some life-altering distractions to keep me occupied for the next few weeks. Henry's thoughts stay with me: *no compromise or regret*. Then I can consider registering for my PhD courses.

I still think about Henry every day. I still ache for him, but my life moves on without him. For instance, today is the day I start running again. This is the best way for me to get back on track. It requires the least amount of thought. I finish tying my running shoes and zip up my hoodie. With my earbuds under my running hat, I crank up the volume and head out the door. Sweat can be a cure-all. At least, that's what I keep telling myself.

Port Washington is breathtaking this time of year. The streets are lined with a technicolor blanket of fallen leaves. The century-old homes are adorned with pumpkins and cornucopias for the impending holidays. As I get closer to the pier, I pass the farmers' market, and the smell of the fresh-baked goods makes me feel fuzzy. It triggers in me a desire for home and normalcy. I can see the pier light at the end of the strip, and I sprint it out, my legs and lungs burning. I pass the pier. This is where I was supposed to stop, but I just keep racing past, urging my body onward. It's like I don't even feel my legs anymore, just the wind in my face and the pounding of my heart saying, *This is the fastest you've ever run.*

Then something snaps, breaks loose. My lungs cry for air, and I slow to a jog then a walk. I drop to my knees. The emotional shackles that have bound me so tightly have finally snapped. The monster is free, and there is nothing I can do to control it. I evacuate a riotous cry. The release is atrocious. It's a contaminated mixture of angst and salvation. The build-up comes pouring out, and I don't care if anyone is watching. I pound the concrete with my fists. Every hyperventilating wail is matched with a blow to the ground.

Without control over my mind or body, my voice drops to a whisper. "Why me? Why me?" I'm so . . . lonely. It feels as though no one else understands what

I'm going through. Of course, I know that isn't true, but it still feels that way. Every comforting word, every let's-act-normal text message—nobody has anything to say that can *make it better*.

My trudge home is ponderous and teary. All I can think about are the nights alone. Empty beds. Dinner tables set for one. Going to the movies alone. When I am finally in the confines of my mother's home, I sink into the couch. There might as well be a chalk outline around the area where my limp body has been stationed for the last couple of weeks.

Get up. Enough's enough.

I think it's time to make a move—after I shower, of course. This not-showering business is getting out of hand.

I head for the bathroom, leaving a trail of workout clothes behind me. My metaphorical molting has begun. The water is probably too hot, but I don't care. It's purifying. I scrub every inch of my body and massage Mom's organic eucalyptus shampoo deep into my scalp. It tingles. At least twenty-five minutes later, I turn the water off and grab one of Mom's fluffy towels.

Mmm . . . This is what home smells like.

My trail of clothes has been picked up, and there is a fresh batch folded on my bed.

Seriously, I don't know how this woman does it. I'm going to treat her to a nice dinner out then break the news to her that I'm going back to Chicago in the morning.

Dried and dressed, I walk into the kitchen. She's sitting at the table with her pre-dinner cup of tea. I head straight for her and lean down and hug her.

She pats my head and coos, "That's a nice welcome, sweetie."

"Thanks for everything, Mom. For who you are and who you taught me to be. For loving me and disciplining me, and for helping me find strength, and most of all, because I am sorry."

Mom makes me stand straight so she can look at me and grabs my hands. "Sorry for what, darling?"

"I'm sorry I didn't appreciate all of this, that I had to hit bottom to realize how incredible you have always been. I'm so proud you are my mother."

"Oh, my sweet girl. You don't have to thank me. This is what we do for our children.

You'll know what I mean one day. What happens to us doesn't define us. It's how we rise after we fall that builds our character." She holds my arms out straight and assesses me from head to toe. "You're going to be just fine, because you are one-hundred percent your mother's daughter."

I give her a loving smile. "Thank goodness, because God knows where I'd be if I wasn't.

Now, go get gussied up. I'm taking you out for dinner."

She beams and practically prances off to get ready. Taking Mom out tonight and celebrating what a positive influence she has been on me is my path back to normalcy. I think I'm ready to move on.

□ □ □

The next night, back in the loft, I begin to unpack my clothes. I only intended to stay a few days with Natalie, then I was going to book into a suites hotel until I got my living arrangements sorted out. Bo offered me the house until it sells, but I'd rather not go back.

Natalie freaked when I told her my plans. She had an extra dresser and bed delivered to the loft. One of her interior designer friends came over, rearranged her bedroom, and hung a glamorous iridescent curtain across the room, so we could both be in there with a little bit of privacy. It looks like I'm here to stay for a while.

After I settle into my new spot in the bedroom, I head back down with the book that I've tried to start reading five times in the last few weeks. I finally have a clear mind. I have cried all I can cry. I have asked "why?" a million times over. The only thing left to do is move on like my mother—run like hell to a new, better life. A glass of prosecco in hand, I curl at my end of the sofa and begin to read.

Nat comes barreling out of the bathroom, looking her fabulous Saturday-night self, and plops down beside me. "Are you sure you don't want to come out with me?"

"I'm sure. A quiet weekend back in my city is exactly what the doctor ordered."

She processes my response for a minute. "You know what? I'm going to stay home too."

"No, you don't have to do that!"

"I know. I want to."

We bundle ourselves up under one of Nat's softest blankets and put on—of all things— the fireplace channel. Cuddled together toe to toe, we gossip and giggle like we used to at slumber parties in seventh grade, with the moon hanging high, gleaming through the windows.

"You know that saying," Nat says, between sips, "that your best friends are the sisters you get to choose in life? Jones, I will always choose you over anything else in this world."

And right there is the clarity I've been craving for weeks shining brighter than a beacon—I'll never be alone.

20

"... good night noises everywhere. The end."

"Okay, children, let's all give Izabel a big, warm thank you for coming in and reading to us today."

The children all yell in unison, "Thank you, Izabel!" They scatter and, facing the vacant semi-circle, I am prompted to stand and gather my things.

"Izabel, thank you so much for volunteering your time. You have no idea how much this means to the children. They just want to lead a normal life like everyone else." Mrs. Kennedy gives me a gracious smile.

"Anytime, Mrs. Kennedy, really. I enjoy being here and seeing them smile."

I'm indebted to Dr. Kennedy for introducing me to his wife. Volunteering here has been the single greatest experience of my life—especially my life post-marriage. It gives me pause to think that I might never have ended up here, might never have volunteered, or only would have shown up to do a photo shoot: "Governor's Wife Visits Terminal Ward at Children's Hospital."

But I love making these kids happy. It's corny but true. They have so much to teach me about life. The first few times, I cried in the bathroom when I had finished reading. But then I met Alexandra. She said, "Bravery is like a fire. The more we feed it, the more it spreads." I feed off their bravery, and I hope they feed off mine, whatever I have to give.

It's cold, but the walk home is refreshing. When I enter the loft, Natalie is splayed on the sofa with a pretty brunette. They both stand to greet me. I drop my bag and walk over to say hello.

"Jones, I'd like you to meet Evangeline. She's an artist visiting from Italy."

I extend my arm to shake her hand. "It's a pleasure to meet you, Evangeline."

Her hair is lush and dark and falls in perfect waves down her shoulders. She's wearing a fitted sweater-dress that accentuates every perfect curve, and over-the-knee stiletto boots. Her big, black eyes complement the pink hue on her cheeks, and her eyelashes go on for miles. Leave it to Natalie to bring home the gorgeous tourist.

"Jones is my very best friend. We're sisters, actually. Will you be in Chicago long, Evangeline?" I ask.

"*Si.* I will be here for a . . . *come si dice, due settimane* . . . a two weeks."

"Well, you have found a perfect tour guide in Natalie. She knows every corner of this city." I look over at Natalie and she blows me a kiss in thanks. We stand quietly for a moment. I am the proverbial third wheel.

"Well, I'm going to wash up, then I have to head out again. It was nice to meet you, Evangeline. I hope you have a wonderful time here in Chicago."

"*Grazie.*" How does she make one simple word sound so sensual?

A few moments later, Nat is on my heels, following me to the bathroom.

"Hi. She's hot, huh?" She's in my face, grinning like—what's that cliché about the cat and the canary? Whatever it is, I can see the feathers dangling from her lips.

"Very. If I was going to have sex with a woman, I would want her to look like that." The word *yes* hisses out from between her teeth as she fist-pumps the air. "Honestly, when did you have time to meet her? I was only gone for a few hours."

"This morning at the bakery. We started talking and found out we're both artists, so I invited her up. So, you don't mind going back out, do you?"

I sigh and shake my head. "No. I can go to a coffee shop. I want to go over my curriculum anyway. But . . . what about Portia?" Instantly, I regret the question. Expressionless, she shrugs, and I know not to inquire further. But the damage is done. Henry has sprung to mind and the image of his lovely face swims in front of my eyes.

With our wordless agreement, she retreats back to the sofa, and I close the door to the bathroom. I wash my face, brush out my hair, and throw it back up into a bun. I take a minute to examine my face. I hope the lighting in here is bad because I look like hell. I pinch my cheeks to get some color. I'll have to get Nat to take me for a primping again. I giggle as I remember the little Filipino lady flipping me around like I was a pancake.

I take a final look in the mirror. "This'll have to do."

As I walk back into the living area, I see that the girls have become much cozier. That's my cue to snag my coat and my backpack and head for the door.

I rustle around the hallway to make enough noise before shouting out, "I'm leaving now." I see a raised hand. Is that a wave? A shoo? Am I even being acknowledged?

Evangeline says something in Italian that I can't make out but clearly understand. *Note to self: call before coming back.* Nat may be busy for a while.

I decide to walk over to Roscoe Village. It seems like that's all I've been doing these days. It has proven to be another form of positive therapy. I take my time strolling through the village in the chilled but bright December sunshine.

Christmas is here next week, and the shop windows are colorfully decorated with Santas, angels, and blinking lights. There are train tracks and nutcrackers in some, and garland and hanging balls in others. The pedestrian traffic is frantic. Shoppers are bustling, carrying bags and packages of varying sizes.

I drop a folded bill into the donation bubble in front of the Salvation Army man, and he tips his hat to me. I'm halted by the carolers singing "God Rest Ye Merry Gentlemen" on the street corner. They're all dressed in period clothing: cloaks and bonnets and top hats. I'm reminded of Mom and me replaying Nana Mouskouri's Christmas CD over and over again for the entire month. I still play it every year.

Of course, this year Christmas will be very quiet, just me and Mom. Natalie has decided to go south to some resort. I checked it out online—looks very hedonistic. That doesn't surprise me one bit. Sometimes, I think I should've taken her up on her offer to go, but I wouldn't want Mom to be alone.

For the last few years, she came to the Carmichaels' estate with Bo and me. Tippy sure does know how to throw a party. Between family, friends, and colleagues there were always at least a hundred people milling about. The first year I was so overwhelmed, but I got used to it. She made all the servers wear elf costumes, which I'm sure they hated, but it always made the guests smile.

Even with all of Tippy's extravagance, nobody could ever accuse her of not being generous. She takes pride in her charities. Instead of handing out gifts, she had a Santa walk around with a big red bag. The guests would have to reach in and choose a small gift box. Inside each box was a receipt for a donation made to a good cause. I hope Bo will be able to enjoy himself this year.

The carolers switch to "Deck the Halls" as clouds roll over and the chill sets in. I should head into the coffee shop. I still have a few hours to waste.

I zip my jacket all the way up and head across the street. It's packed when I get there, with hardly a seat to be found. I scoot over to the only one I can find and claim it with my jacket and bag. The lineup is just as crazy. Everybody's ordering Peppermint Kisses and Cinnamon Snowflakes—or whatever all those sugary Christmas specials are called. I just want my regular-non-fat vanilla latte.

Back in my chair and armed with my coffee, I pull

out the application forms the university mailed to me and begin to flip through the literature. I've thought about going back to school for months now. If I want to start classes in the fall, I'll have to have my registration completed by early February, which isn't much time, considering all that goes into them.

My phone buzzes in my pocket. The coast is clear already? I look at the screen but don't recognize the number.

"This must be some sort of record. Are you done already, Nat?"

"Jones?"

I freeze, and nervous exhilaration takes over my body. Tears immediately build at the backs of my eyes.

"Henry . . ." My voice is cracked and hoarse.

"How's Chicago?"

"Okay," is all I can think to say. He doesn't respond. "Treating me better these days," I feel compelled to add.

"I see. I hope he's treating you better too." His response makes me nervous. I can hear the hurt and the tinge of anger under the would-be cool and collectedness. "I'm sorry. I shouldn't have sa—"

"No, Henry. I'm sorry. I—I didn't go back to him. It's over between us. It was over that day." I want to scream that I tried to call and explain, that I just wanted to prevent a fight, that I needed to face him on my own. A long silence occupies our air space. I can feel his breath on my neck through the phone.

"How are you?" I ask as generic a question as possible or I'll break down right here in the coffee shop.

"I miss you, Izabel Jones."

There's nothing to keep my tears at bay. "I miss you too." I swallow back a sob.

"I need to see you again. These past few weeks have been the worst of my life. I owe you an explanation." He pauses. "I owe you an apology."

I wipe the tears off my eyes and face with the cuff of my hoodie. "Okay. Yes, I would like that very much."

I hear him release a big sigh as if he's been holding his breath the entire time. "I'm so happy you said that, Jones."

The buzz in the coffee shop disappears. It goes completely quiet as I slip into a state of total euphoria at the thought of seeing him again. I'm pressing my phone against my ear, my eyes closed, thinking of wrapping my arms around him.

"When do you want to meet?" I ask. "How about right now?"

My eyes spring open. He's here.

"Henry!"

Acknowledgments

Thank you to my husband for your patience and for never questioning me when I jump off the cliff without a second thought.

To my children for giving me the love and inspiration that I crave every day. I love you! To my parents, who taught me to never give up and that nothing is unattainable.

To my sister for always being there for me, lending me an ear, and always having my back.

To my brother, who inadvertently taught me how to escape every wrestling move when we were young.

To my beautiful girlfriends, thank you for keeping grounded.

To Nikki Bettinelli, my PR Maven, "The Boss of me," my cheerleader. A crazy idea brought us together, and now our wonderful friendship will keep us together. I couldn't imagine taking this journey without you.

To Elyse Gagne, thank you for fixing my many mistakes.

To my new "A" team at Hadleigh House Publishing. Thank you for taking a chance on me. I look forward to a long and prolific friendship.

To my Krissy, I've loved you since we were fourteen years old. Without you, this story would never have come to life. You are the epitome of resilience.

About JB Lexington

JB Lexington is a romance writer based out of Toronto, Ontario. *Forever Eve* is her first novel, and she is currently working on a sequel.

JB lives with her husband, two kids, and two dogs. When she isn't writing she can be found at the gym, strolling designer boutiques in her neighborhood, or sipping a glass of pinot grigio at a local restaurant.

www.readjb.com